THE EMENTHIAN

Sylas Seabrook

Bookish Nerds Publishing LLC

bookishnerds.com

MEDALLION ARTWORK BY
Sabreen Massey

EDITED BY
Victoria McAvoy

SENSITIVITY READER
E.A. Noble

For information on other publications by the author, visit
https://sylas.art

ISBN 978-1-963623-04-8 (paperback)
ISBN 978-1-963623-03-1 (e-book)

For Dustin Craig, who stands as a tower of inspiration and support in my life.

Acknowledgments

The Ementhian was made better by the contributions of many others. Without their input, this novel would not be what it is today. A special thanks goes to Dustin Craig for all of his patience in listening and advising me while developing and writing.

To my editor, Victoria McAvoy, thank you for helping perfect the grammar and punctuation, making sure that the story accurately conveys my intentions.

Thank you to my alpha readers who advised on a rough version of this work:

Mel Friday, whose sky-high take on the story ensures its overall flow and consistency;

Joseph Hand, whose comprehensive, detailed, and critical analysis refines the manuscript and reveals its true message; and

Cheryl Sims, who applies an experienced eye toward ensuring the overall flow stays on track.

Orion Lee for his continued support and honest feedback. He's been there from the beginning.

To my beta readers, thank you as well. Your contributions helped refine this work into a polished piece. Beta reader Dahlia MacEachern is a testament to excellence and thoroughness—her feedback has been fundamental and is truly appreciated. Madison Jacobs' early take was very helpful and appreciated; she's a great supporter who I look forward to hearing more from. A special thank you to Austin Jennison—a beta reader I forgot in my last book!—whose thoroughness and questioning eye ensures every sentence conveys its intended meaning.

Content Advisory

This book contains content not suitable for all ages. Sensitive topics include violence, suicidal behavior, and references to underage sex. If these topics are not for you, please select another work for your reading enjoyment.

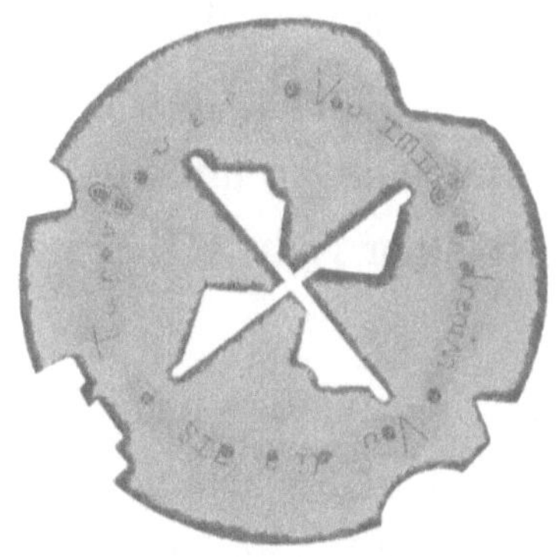

TRIBINIUS CANTUS

Ahnd adjusted the camera's audio, filtering out cars blaring music and the thumping of the club in the background. He tweaked the lighting, then grinned. Hell yeah. He was ready. He held up his fingers to count down from three, then rolled the title sequence. As the intro streamed, tens of thousands of eager viewers across the planet tuned in, waiting for the star of the show.

Three.

Two.

One.

The opening sequence segued, bringing into view the guy standing in front of Ahnd's camera, his best friend and captain of the team. Six-feet-tall and strapped in a tight fitting Inves suit that formed against a firm abdomen with teal streams of flowing vapor lining the seams, Tribinius smiled, the purplish-red, heart-shaped birthmark on his cheekbone perking up. The bump in numbers and burst of chat in the stream confirmed that girls everywhere were falling for that smile. Tribinius was in his element. Ahnd was proud to be the guy behind the camera, the one who brought Tribinius' view of himself to life.

"Hey, friends," Tribinius said as his Adori—a small fluffy robotic bird—reached around and pecked the side of his face. "It's Trib, and I hope you're ready for another episode of *Can't Stop The Trib*. You guessed it—there's no stopping me today."

He raised his brows and cast a curious glance to his right with a devilish grin. "Are we going in there?"

Ahnd panned the camera to follow Trib's eyes and brought the Lucky Lady, a dance club known for its private shows, into view. It sported a glowing red neon sign of a topless dancing woman hanging alongside the two-story building. The second story was lit up like an office with a bright window in the middle. A burly bouncer guarding the ground door stared at them with a blank face and solid posture, oblivious to Trib's dramatic presentation, but the shadows of the night fell across him like a dangerous omen. A short line of patrons waited to enter, raising the sleeve of their Inveses to let him scan their IDs.

"Nope," Trib said, reaching out and pulling the camera back to him. Swinging his arm out like the presenter he was, he rotated around, directing the camera across the Myeinth cityscape, buildings towering in the city's blue haze, and up to the peak of Ementhe Tower. The building rose 150 stories above the city like a spire of power, its features edged with teal vapor lights pulsing like an artery. "We're setting our sights higher. My dad's office."

Ahnd zoomed back, focusing on the lip-biting Trib, then expanding the view to take in Trib's torso.

"This is going to get me in trouble, but we're going to paint the sky colors. You ready to go where no man has gone before?" Trib snickered. "No, my dad doesn't count."

Cocking his head to the side and swooping his arm forward, he said, "Come on. Let's go."

They rushed down the street the two blocks to Ementhe Tower, garbage, and a light vapor under foot. Trib's artificial legs propelled him along faster than Ahnd's natural legs, making Ahnd trail his friend. Ahnd released a little vapor from his suit and his camera lifted in front of him, floating and keeping steady as they ran.

At D&N's, a dilapidated but heavily lit day and night shop, Trib spun around, letting Ahnd catch up and the camera bring him into full view. Unlike Ahnd, he didn't have to catch his breath. It helped to be half machine.

Trib threw his arms down and pumped vapor through his suit. The suit lit up, glowing like an overworked neon sign as he swung his arm around and pointed to a door in the next building over, Ementhe Tower.

"That's the dungeon, AKA the mailroom. We start there, then it's up to the top." He spun his head around and his body followed in a sweet spin. His short, brown hair tumbled around his head as it reflected the glow of his suit. He bolted for the door, making his Adori flap its wings and fight to keep its balance as it gripped tightly.

At the door, he stopped abruptly, Ahnd halting a short distance away, carefully choreographed to listen in. A black-haired girl stood in front of the door, eyes speaking disaffection, posture denying belief, and curls at the end of her hair bobbing like they had somewhere better to be. She looked at her fingernails, rubbed one against her shirt, and nodded.

"I've heard better stories. What makes you think I'm going to let you do an idiot thing like this?"

Trib laughed, picked her up, and set her on the ground behind him.

"Because you can't stop the Trib." He cocked his head to the side with no small degree of confidence and circled back around to the door.

"Tribinius Cantus! How dare you? I'm not something you can just pick up and throw around."

"I didn't throw you," he said, peeking over his shoulder. "I set you down gently. Now, what's the code, trixer? You've got tricks to get you through anything in the matrix."

She pursed her unbelieving lips, shook her head, then mouthed the code, keeping it secret from the audience.

"Thanks, Liv," he said, raising the edge of his smile and driving girls wild.

Liv laughed. "I would never try to actually stop you, but that was a good act, wasn't it?"

"Perfect," he said, popping open the door. "Ready for act two?"

"Mhmm."

Ahnd rolled his eyes but kept the camera rolling. She had it bad for him. That was tough for her. Trib would never settle with a girl. He'd convinced himself that since he was bipolar, it wasn't in the cards.

They entered the mailroom, Ahnd following closely behind as he adjusted the camera with a lighting filter to give it an eerie feeling. The room was filled with tables covered in boxes and stacks of unopened mail while metal cabinets that hadn't been opened in ages lined the walls. The metallic gray of the room reflected the light mist of vapor that crept like a living haze across the floor while dust motes twinkled in the light of broken, flashing lights hanging overhead.

"They say that what goes in the mailroom stays in the mailroom. I've never actually seen anyone working down here," Trib said, eyes wide open and glowing ghostly in the mist. "There are many elevators in this building, but only one that leads directly to where we're going. That elevator is over here," he whispered as he hesitantly pointed, stirring the dust into a tempest behind his arm.

Ahnd grinned. His buddy was such a showman. The performance was enough to make him think it was a haunted mailroom.

Inside the elevator, Ahnd lowered the camera to his waist and aimed it up at Trib, the overhead view port on the camera letting him watch the shot. He noticed the stream stats and nodded with appreciation. Signing 100 to Trib, Trib leaned into the camera.

"Ahnd says we just hit 100,000 viewers! Let's make it a million. You're going to love this. I'm going to jump off the tower! And who do you think is going to stop me?"

Trib laughed, then watched the floor numbers as they ascended. Ahnd drew the camera around to focus on the display. As they approached 150, he turned the camera back to Trib.

Trib held out his hand and with pomp and circumstance, his head high and haughty. "The code, please, Livia."

She slapped him on the chest, causing the Adori, to flap its wings and squawk. "I didn't print it."

"Why not?" Trib asked, relaxing his posture with faux disappointment. He reached up and rubbed the bird's neck. "It's ok, Peetie. That would have been so cool, Liv." He shrugged and the elevator door opened, exposing an inner locked door. "Okay, the code, please?"

She shook her head, reached forward and pushed in the 24 digit code.

"Damn, dad," Trib said as the steel door slid open. "Who has that long of a password?"

Trib spun around and threw his hands up, blocking the exit. "As a descendent of Alexander Reyes and heir to Ementhe Enterprises, I welcome you to my future office. Please, make yourself at home."

With that, he threw his arm in a smooth motion only possible with prosthetics. Pointing at the room, the camera zoomed past him and into the office. Everything was rich...and black. From the high-backed cowhide chair, which was backwards as if his father had been looking behind him when he left, to the desk made of some black crystal Ahnd couldn't identify, to the plush couches and fine art, everything was expensive. And black.

Trib twirled into the room as if he owned the place, stopping facing a wall, and grinned.

"Ah, and here it is. My inheritance. It's said that the person who possesses this owns Ementhe Enterprises," Trib said, drawing attention to a medallion hanging in a sealed glass case. "Don't be fooled. It's heavily protected. If I tried to take that, all hell would come down on us before we could escape."

Ahnd cammed around and focused on the medallion. It was circular, with odd asymmetric patterns cut out of the edges. The face contained etching that looked like words in a language Ahnd didn't recognize. Were they even words?

Trib shrugged. "It's kind of ugly. I can wait. How many are we at?"

Ahnd checked the display and snorted. "500."

"Perfect. Halfway there. Let's go out on the balcony," Trib said. "It's time to light up the night sky."

Suddenly, the black chair behind the desk spun around. A man as tall as Trib with a lot of wrinkles, peppered hair pulled back exposing a widow's peak, a gray mustache and goatee, and beady aged eyes sat in the chair, arms relaxing in his lap, peering down at Trib through spectacles.

"I don't think you will," he said, his voice as crackly as his aged skin.

Trib jerked around and pointed at the man. "What are *you* doing here?"

"In my office? What kind of question is that?"

A side door opened and three security guards entered, fanning out.

"Stop him," the old man said.

"Go, Trib!" Liv yelled. Taking her cue, she ran out of the door to escape the building. She was never intended to follow Trib where he was going next.

Trib shook his head, then looked straight at the camera. "Can't stop the Trib," he yelled. He grabbed a Mæssation Corporation vapor disk hanging from the side of his Inves, centered the vehicle-spawning device in his hand, then pumped vapor from his suit into it. It lit up with traces of teal light that emanated from the disk out into the model of a hoverboard on the balcony. Liv took the hint and opened the door while Ahnd powered up his own Mæssan and a second hoverboard appeared in the office a distance behind Trib's.

The guards rushed toward Trib, giving Ahnd a chance to perform his secondary role for Trib: security guard. He rushed forward and shoulder shoved the back guard, causing the man to tumble forward into another guard, then hopped on his Mæssan hoverboard as the light solidified. The third guard looked back at the ruckus, and Ahnd crouched, extending his arm and clipping the guard at the knees.

This gave Trib the chance he needed, and he ran forward as his Mæssan hardened, then leaped on it while Peetie hunkered down, wings spread as if ready to fly the hoverboard itself. His feet locked in place, Trib leaned back and the board shot forward, lifting into the air. Ahnd was close behind him. Trib flew out about forty feet, then leaned on his back foot, sending his board almost vertical.

Ahnd lifted the camera, steadied it with some vapor,

and continued broadcasting Tribinius' insane moves.

Wind rushed through Tribinius's hair, pulling it back and driving him forward. The rush of power, confidence, and purpose overtook him. He was king of the world, master of his universe, awesomeness itself. He modulated his suit's vapors, mixing them in a magical array and making a rainbow of colors as he pumped them out, drawing "Tribinius" in flowing script accented with a swirl underneath behind him. This should get him to his million viewers.

He curved his board around and charged directly at Ahnd with his hand in the air, then caught something in his peripheral vision at the corner of an alley about a block down the street from the D&N, kitty corner from the Lucky Lady. Was that what he thought? Did that man just hit that woman? Oh, no, he didn't. Trib was already higher than high, both literally and figuratively, but now, something flowed through him like an unbridled fury. He forgot his achievement, his purpose, and started breathing hard. Like a whirlwind plucking him out of the sky, his focus stolen, his mind became a blank wall of thought flooded with emotion. He set his jaw tight. The man was some gigantic beast with jacked up ears. *How dare he hit a woman? He'll do it again. He'll...*Trib's thoughts shattered and emotion drove him like a catatonic engine of determination.

Can't stop the Trib flittered through his mind like a propellant forcing him forward. It was his last thought before he angled his feet, pulling in at a sharp curve, and headed straight for the man. He reached down and streamed some vapor directly from his natural Innie reserves, pumping vapor into his board as he depleted his suit. Blind, thoughtless rage driving him, the vapor poured from his reserves—a reserve bigger than what most had—streaming from his fingertips into the hoverboard and taking him to a dangerous speed. He was about to show this jerk why you can't stop the Trib.

In the distance, he heard Ahnd's worried yell, but his numbed state of mind didn't catch the words.

The jerk turned just as Trib came down level with him. He puffed his chest up and raised his arms. As Trib charged, the man's arms came down and crashed into the board.

Trib went flying and Peetie shot into the air. Tumbling was more like it, but he didn't lose his focus or his fury. He threw out his hands and fired a bolt of Innie vapor into the pavement, causing the vapor to thicken and slow his descent. He landed on his feet, surrounded by arches of solidified Ementhium. Breaking free of his vapor safety net, he turned around and sneered at the enormous man with cauliflower ears.

"What do you think you're doing, asshole?" Trib said.

The man waved Trib forward. Well, he was asking for

it. Trib ran forward, building up a reserve of Innie vapor, and when he got near the man, raised his arm, ready to slam it into the man's chest, but the unseemly man had longer arms. It caught Trib off guard. Trib was six feet tall with prosthetic arms. Who had arms longer than....The behemoth grabbed Trib by the neck and spun him around, slamming Trib against the wall in one swift motion.

It happened fast and hard. Trib was winded before he knew it, his energetic vapor misting away in a big cloud.

"You made me lose my girl. I guess you're going to have to take her place," the man growled.

"Damn, Trib. Why picking him?" Ahnd said, skating in on his board and coming to a rapid rest. "Know those ears?"

"What?" Trib said, shrugging and trying to regain his breath. The bully clenched his fist tighter.

"Look. Arrange something. Don't hurt my friend," Ahnd said.

"You going to take *her* place?"

"Trib!" Liv screamed, running up. "Let him go!"

"Got money. Can pay. Buy one," Ahnd said.

"Yeah. I do," Trib eked out. There was something about getting the wind knocked out of you that weakened the feelings of being a god, but despite that, Trib still wanted to show this monster up. He would figure that out in time, but right now his chest hurt and his neck was no better. Trib was inclined to use his mechanical arms to grab the man, but with the grip on his neck, he'd suffer a crushed windpipe before he managed a scratch.

Five cars rolled into place. Calmly. Doors opened, and eighteen suited and well-armed men stepped out, drawing weapons. The hum of the weapons powering up echoed down a street which was suddenly silent except for the club's thumping. From the lead car, the driver's door opened, and a man stepped out. His angular, serious face spoke business while his formality spoke professionalism. His posture and build said well-trained and lethal. He calmly fixed his suit, straightened his tie, and walked up to the beast still holding Trib by the neck.

"I'll take charge of this one," he said, looking the man in the face, his eyes as cold as the man's grip was firm.

The man snorted.

"When I say, take out his kneecaps and elbows," the suited man said loud enough for the armed militia behind him to hear. Guns clicked and the men re-aimed.

The suited man turned a plain face toward the beast holding Trib. "The deal is, you keep your body parts, and I get him. Do we have a deal?"

"Pej, shoot him. He's going to kill me," Trib said.

Trib's plea didn't help.

The cauliflower-eared man squeezed Trib's neck harder, then flung his arm to the right, throwing Trib to the ground. He grumbled as he faced Pej and tapped him twice on the chest. "I'll remember this."

"Get in the car," Pej said without looking at Trib.

Trib rubbed his neck, then noticed someone watching. Above the Lucky Lady, a shadowed figure watched the scene. He turned his back and walked away, leaving the window a bright spot in a dark night. Trib climbed to his feet, bowed his head, huffing, and stomped off to the cars.

"Got a mill," Ahnd said.

A million viewers. He'd done it. Exactly what he'd planned. Even a big brute couldn't stop him. Trib shook his head and looked at Ahnd, the camera aimed directly at him. It boosted his ego again, and he smiled, lifting his head high. "Can't stop the Trib!"

He grinned as Ahnd turned the camera up at the sky, Liv behind Ahnd and the vapors still lighting it up with Trib's name.

DOCTOR MUTHILI

The office was as sterile as a mental hospital and Doctor Muthili's advice as bland as the food. Light tan walls gave the room a depressing feeling while the plain furniture instilled a feeling of disaffection. It didn't help that the singsong drone of the doctor's voice was like a Siren leading you to doom.

Trib stood at the window, unfocused eyes taking in a blur of pastel walls. The doctor's office was on the inside of the building facing the inner courtyard. There was greenery below, which should have cheered him up, but today it would take more than grass and trees to liven him up. Even the massive glass tube funneling Ementhium from deep within the Earth's core didn't impress Trib; it felt like a drone pounding down his hopes.

He had gone from feeling on top of the world to getting the wind knocked out of him, and somehow coming down from that height hit him harder than it should. Or did it? The higher you were, the harder the fall, right? The thing about everyone thinking you're bipolar is that everything you do is seen through that colored lens. You can't just have a good day or a bad day, you have bipolar days. It wasn't like that in truth. Bipolar people have good days and bad days, just like normal people. If he was being honest with himself, though, the brute was a trigger. The question was if it triggered a bipolar moment or if it was a reasonable moment.

What would a reasonable guy do when he saw another guy hitting a woman? Would he stand by and do nothing? That didn't seem very reasonable to Trib. Yes, the guy had triggered him, but Trib didn't even believe he was bipolar. This had to be a case of a reasonable reaction to a violent scene, right?

"You don't understand me. No one does," Trib said, his voice as hollow as his stare.

The doctor's ensuing silence was irritating, but Trib felt the need to explain.

"I don't remember getting triggered by the guy. No, I didn't think about it. It's like a fire that burns through your brain and makes you want to scream, but it's not just raging, it's giving you orders. It's like you're turning into chaos, but at the same time, you feel totally in charge. It doesn't matter. You don't care. No one cares."

"I do care, Tribinius. That's why we're here."

"No, we're here because I lost my shit again and

almost got hurt, so my dad wants you to give me more medication. I'm sixteen. How much crap are you going to pump into me?"

"I'm going to do it. I'm going to be king of the world."

Trib frowned and wished the male voice in his head would go away. He hadn't heard the female one in a while. Why did he hear voices? It could be worse. They could have a conversation. But maybe it meant the doctors were right and he was 97.5% likely to be bipolar. Trib didn't want to accept that. It would mean he was broken, and he didn't want to be broken. At least he hadn't mentioned the voices to Doctor Muthili. He'd only prescribe more medications.

"I'm not going to give you more medication. Do you think that if you took your meds, this might not have happened?"

"Ninety-seven point five. That's the likelihood that I am bipolar. What about the other 2.5%? What if I'm not bipolar and you just keep giving me all these meds that I don't need? Have you thought about that? Would you have stood by and let him beat that woman? Has anyone asked if what I did was reasonable? No...no, nevermind. It doesn't matter. I don't care. You definitely don't care."

Trib didn't really care. What was there to care about? He felt the urge to plead his case, but at the same time, he didn't care. No one cared about him, so what really mattered anyway?

"You do matter, Tribinius. People do care about you. And you care about them. What about Livia and Ahnd, your friends?"

They would be fine without him. They would continue on. Ahnd was a great guy who would go far if he stayed off the streets, and his camera skills were wicked. Liv was so smart. He was surprised she hadn't gone to Alexandria to become a scientist. She could do anything. But what did Trib have? A sentence. He was sentenced to living in his father's footsteps, no hope of escape. He enjoyed his show. That's what he really wanted to do, but fate wouldn't let him have that. His father was threatening to take it away. It didn't matter. They would all be fine without him.

"So, what do I have to do to get out of here?"

"My office? Walk out the door. No one is keeping you here. But if you're asking what we would like you to do, I'd like you to ask yourself a question: When do you like yourself best?"

He didn't like himself. He was just a showman without much to show, lost in a fate he couldn't control. What was to like? Hell, he didn't even have real arms and legs, and girls only liked him because of his birthmark or money. Sometimes both. He was just a guy with too much vapor and not enough hope.

"I don't."

"You don't ever like yourself?"

"Nope."

"Are you having ideations again?"

"Of suicide? Not yet."

"I want you to take your meds. Will you promise me to do that?"

"I guess."

"Will you promise to tell someone if you have ideations?"

"Yeah. Fine."

The doctor made a few notes, then took a moment to enter Trib's prescriptions. "Is there anything else you would like to talk about?"

"No."

"Then I'll see you in two weeks."

Trib rolled his eyes. Two weeks meant he was in trouble. They were checking that he took his meds. Whatever. It didn't matter.

He turned from the window, nodded at Doctor Muthili, and left, working his way down a hallway with nondescript doors on one side and a line of glass windows on the other showing the tube of Ementhium pumping vapor from the mines below into the engine which was the building. At the end of the hallway next to the elevator was the stairway. It was a long walk. Too much thinking was getting in his way. Did Doctor Muthili really care? No, he couldn't. Trib was just a patient. Any care was superficial. Who really cared about him? Did he really care about himself?

The stairs twisted around in a circle, spiraling down and leaving a space between that was a straight shot. He stepped through the doorway to the stairs, but hesitated. He felt down and an "accidental" fall down the stairs was too easy. The hollow fall through the middle of the stairway was enticing; he could jump. If he landed just right...no, he didn't want to do that. He carefully stepped back, pulling away from his thoughts as much as the stairway, and took the elevator, head lowered as a couple who joined him talked, interested in each other. They had someone who cared about them. Why didn't Trib have anyone who cared about him?

Three psychiatrists served all employees of Ementhe Enterprises, with Doctor Muthili reserved for the executives. Their offices were on the third floor, so at least it was a short trip. Lost in reflection, Trib strolled down the street, past D&N's, past where the man had attacked the woman, past the Lucky Lady, and down yet another block, then crossed the street. He looked both ways, though he wasn't sure why. He had an apartment in the housing complex there, something he kept for himself, away from the mansion his father owned in the suburbs of the rich and famous. That apartment was the Pad, and it was where he, Ahnd, and Liv hung out. At the door, he pressed his palm to the security pad and entered the code as he sighed. Maybe he shouldn't come to them now. Not with how he felt.

It didn't matter, he decided. They wouldn't care anyway.

COUNCILOR CANTUS

In a dark clone of his office on the 150th floor of Ementhe Enterprises, Caran Cantus pressed a button to seal the room, and the door locked with a special mix of vapor. It was virtually impermeable.

A teal hologram splattered into the air in front of him, then spread out and formed the shape of the nine. Everyone but one on the council was a CEO, referred to as a Councilor in this room alone. The last member had not arrived.

Today's pre-meeting discussion was as boring as ever. No one bothered with Councilor Cantus. Usually. A light flashing on his console indicated a signal from Councilor Northund. He was a younger Councilor from Babylon, not fit to address Councilor Cantus.

Caran reached out and pressed the screen to let the call come through, lifting his head high and staring down his nose as Councilor Northund appeared as a holograph in front of him. His snide scowl was almost as perfected as

Caran's. He had apparently picked up some skills lately.

Caran stared at the Councilor.

"Greetings, Councilor Cantus."

"Make your point, not pleasantries."

"Your son's indiscretions are drawing attention."

"He runs a stream. That's the point."

"Not the kind of attention he should be gathering."

"If he was of concern, someone with greater tenure on this council would address me, not you."

"Consider it a kindness, Councilor."

"I didn't ask for kindness. Babylonians talk too much," Caran hissed, then swooped his hand up in a long arc with his finger extended and pressed the button to cancel the hologram.

Caran kept looking forward, waiting for the last member, but noticed Councilor Northund popping up at various desks around the room. Northund was a minion tossed out as a litmus test. Caran curled his upper lip in disgust.

The sphere in the middle of the arc of Councilors lit up, glowing a bright white, then a man in solid white stepped out of the sphere. It was too bright to see him, but their leader had arrived. No one ever saw his face.

"Councilors," a digitally remastered voice boomed from the sphere as the man spoke. The voice was commanding, but gentle. "Let us convene."

The meeting began with the standard complaints. How could they make profits higher? Why wasn't Alexandria treated the same? The questions went on like doldrums to a migraine.

"What about the Cantus boy?" Councilor Plourvald asked.

Councilors peppered the air with grumbles and snorts, but Caran didn't move.

"He is a Trinnie. He cannot cause that much trouble. Leave him for now," the Leader said.

"But—" Councilor Plourvald began, but the sphere brightened and the Leader turned toward Plourvald.

"Meeting adjourned," the Leader said, then stepped back into the sphere. It pulsed with light, then dimmed.

Plourvald stayed as quiet as Caran. Plourvald should learn his place and defer to his elders. In time. Caran had a long-term plan, and something as petty as his son's antics couldn't interfere with them.

THE PAD

Liv was kicked back, feet up on the footrest of her recliner, the whole thing tilted back as she stared into the eyepiece studying code broadcast onto the ceiling. She was fairly certain she needed to shift a byte but hadn't convinced herself. Why was she debating it? She should just test it. She put the bitwise operator in place, then...

The door to the Pad slid open, and she immediately lost focus, flipping the chair into an upright position, taking off the eyepiece, and dropping it in a side pocket.

"Trib! You're back," she said, heading toward him. "I'm so glad...." She stopped. His demeanor was off. He looked downtrodden. "What's wrong?"

"Nothing. It doesn't matter. What's going on?"

"Oh," Liv said. He lacked energy, exuberance. He definitely wasn't himself. He must be feeling down. "Having a hard time? We're here for you."

"Thanks," he said, eyes devoid of passion.

"Million viewers. What's next?" Ahnd said. He was only fifteen, yet a couple inches taller than Trib, and he clearly didn't know how much pain Trib was in. Liv was a year older than Ahnd, but by girls and boys matur.... No. She didn't like that line of thought. It wasn't about gender, it was about Ahnd being clueless. Still, how could he be that daft?

"We'll talk about that later," she said.

Trib sighed and went to the kitchen.

"Ahnd, really? He's feeling depressed. Can't you show some concern for Trib?"

"Show doesn't depress. Gonna snap out of it. Always does. Sooner or later."

Liv shook her head, mouth dropped in disbelief, then joined Trib in the kitchen that was nicer than at home, with a refrigerator that cost as much as all the appliances in her mother's kitchen. It was part of being Trib's friend. What he thought was average was high middle class to the rest of the world.

"Is it bad this time?" she asked.

Trib shrugged, sipping from a soda. "Does it matter? You don't have to care."

"Well, maybe this will cheer you up. Peetie? Come here. Your daddy is home."

Hearing the name, Trib actually smiled. The Adori flew around as he extended a finger, the robotic bird with dragon wings, yet fluffy as a newborn chick, landing on it. He rubbed the back of its neck and the bird pushed into his finger as if it got as much joy from the petting as Trib did.

"There you are. I missed you, little guy. How's my Peetie?"

Livia smiled as she watched him heartened by Peetie.

Peetie craned his neck, fluffing his down up to let Trib' fingers get deep.

"It's good to see you enjoying something."

"Yeah. I guess. At least a robot can love me."

Liv sighed, and Trib looked at her, pain on his face causing a wrinkle to his heart birthmark.

"I'm bringing you down. Can't have that. Don't worry. Can't stop the Trib, right? Come on. Let's go plan the next show," he said, setting the empty can down on the too-nice counter.

The smile he put on was totally staged, yet he caught her with it. She wanted to believe he was okay, even though she knew there was an indescribable pain hidden under his boyish perfection. She returned his smile with her own fake smile, one that said she was happy for him while hiding her own angst.

He rolled to the side, spinning his dejected and pained body around, then headed for the living room. Even the way he moved when he was down was sexy. Liv followed, grabbing the can and putting it in the recycling compactor not two feet from where he set the cup. She'd complain at him except he wouldn't care at the moment, and all she cared about was caring for him.

In the living room, Ahnd had moved from his recliner—they all had one in a makeshift circle in the center of the room—to his desk against the beige wall. He didn't look up, but said, "What's next? Skydiving?"

"Not a bad idea," Trib said with playfulness. "No chute?"

That earned raised brows from Ahnd. "Ground can stop the Trib. Hard, bro."

Trib laughed. "Okay, so that's out. What's in?"

"What about something that uses your vapors? All of them," Liv suggested.

Trib threw his head back, totally humored, and stared at her, lips pursed. "What would do that?"

Liv shrugged. She was just coming up with ideas. She didn't really have one, but it would be cool. Then it came to her. "What about catching a Vapor?"

That got both of the boys' attention. There were ten types of vapors. Nine of them were actual vapors, produced in each city that powered technology. Some people were even born with their own ability to control a vapor. A few people could use two vapors. They were called Binnies. Trib could use three, making him a Trinnie.

He was extremely rare (and not just for his good looks). She'd only ever heard of one person using more than three. That was Alexander Reyes, the discoverer of the vapors—he could use all nine. The tenth was a creature made of vapors. Vapor leaked around cities, forming a light tint to the air. Ementhium was light blue with a touch of green, so Myeinth was a constant ethereal blue tint, but wherever people used vapors, vapor escaped. It would pool, form eddies, and if enough came together, it would form a ghost, an almost living apparition. With a bit of Tituerium vapor, the ghost could be given life. These living ghosts were called Vapors.

"Dangerous," Ahnd said.

"Perfect. Let's do it. What should it look like?" Trib said.

"A snake." Ahnd's chuckle was devious. He was a rough boy for his age, but that came from his childhood.

"A cat. Like a leopard." Liv suggested.

"Can't have it eating Peetie," Trib said, shaking his head. Peetie craned around and nipped at Trib's ear. Trib laughed affectionately at Peetie's approval. Adoris were linked to their owners on a physical level, and Peetie was probably sending an emotion of pleasure to its master. Good. Trib needed something pleasurable.

Liv's thoughts about Trib's pleasure made her blush.

Trib raised a finger in a comical fashion—like a cartoon where the protagonist just uncovered the solution. "A transformer! I'll... I'll bind it to... um, Peetie."

Peetie nipped at Trib's ear again, causing him to yelp and grab his ear. "What? You don't want to become a cassowary?"

Peetie cocked his head to the side.

"It's the most dangerous bird to humans, but no, you're too cute to be a cassowary. Let's see. Jankus, what is the most dangerous flying bird on Earth?"

A circular disk about two inches tall came to life and shot a holographic face up above it, radiating out from the center. It blinked and smiled as its software loaded. "It is good to see you too, sir. I assume by your conversation that you do not want any of the top three birds, since you have rejected the cassowary. Perhaps the lammergeir, also called the bearded vulture, is more suited to your taste."

Jankus generated another hologram in front of him, a bird with a curved beak, golden head and body, and black and white feathers covering its wings. It was about three feet tall and four feet long. The bird extended its wings and Trib naturally ducked as it spread out farther than he was tall.

"That's perfect, right Peetie?"

Peetie chirped submissively and rubbed its head on Trib's shoulder.

"That settles it," Trib said. "Peetie's going to be a

bearded vulture Vapor transformer.”

Liv laughed. “You think you can do that? Do you know your vapors that well?”

Trib shrugged. “What’s going to stop me from trying?”

“Got your back, but dangerous. Vapors attack,” Ahnd said, staring at the holographic bird.

“And that’s exactly why it’s going to get us up to two million views,” Trib said.

“Tribinius Cantus,” Liv said in a motherly voice. “If you’re dead, you’ll have no views.”

Trib patted her on the head. Patted her on the head! Who did he think he was?

“It’ll be okay, Liv. I’ve got this. And you do a horrible job of mimicking my mother’s voice.”

He laughed, perking his smile up at the edges, and winked at her, his birthmark heart seeming to wink along with him. She would blush if he hadn’t just patted her on the head. She was his age. Where did he think he was getting off?

Liv donned a smile intended to look fake and cocked her head to the side, as condescending as she could be, then said absolutely nothing. It was a woman’s right to confuse men, and he had just earned his punishment.

Frustratingly, he ignored her, focusing instead on the task at hand.

"Okay, so Ahnd, we need to find a place with the right vapor mix and get our timing right. That's on you," he said, then faced her with his boyish smile. "Liv, I need you to take care of Peetie. Give him to me at just the right moment."

"But you have to make sure you can do it. How are you going to do that?"

"I'm going to see Coach Xius."

"Why not your fath—"

Liv stopped mid-word. The obvious answer coming to her a little slower than the words coming out of her mouth. Of course, he couldn't see his father. His father would just try to stop him. Coach Xius was the one adult Trib trusted.

"Nevermind. When's the show?"

"Two days. That gives you enough time, Ahnd?" Trib said.

Ahnd shrugged. "Yeah. All good."

"I'll pull up a topographical map of the city," Liv said. "That'll let us figure out where vapor should pool."

COACHING

Trib rolled over, his body tender, mind numb, and looked at the clock. It was 3:30, and the sun was out. Had he really slept eighteen hours? He was still so tired. Maybe he should roll back over, bury his head in the pillows, and get some more rest. No. He had somewhere to be. And if he didn't get his butt out of bed, he wouldn't get there in time.

"Handyman, attach right arm," he said.

His arms and legs were hanging from the wall next to his bed, and a machine came to life, its arm turning and grabbing Trib's right arm from storage while another machine propped up Trib. Lasers activated, guiding the machine to place Trib's arm in place, vapor releasing as the prosthetic approached Trib's stump and sealing into place.

Trib reached up and pulled his left arm off the wall and locked it into place, then hopped off the bed, keeping his torso hovering over the floor. Leaning his head back, he let out a massive yawn, then stretched his torso, pulling his senses back into shape. He could wait until tomorrow, couldn't he? He glanced at his bed and felt the ache in his muscles, then shook his head. *Don't let the bed stop you.*

He hopped in the shower to finish waking up, turning the temperature a little too cool. After a vigorous scrubbing, he swung out, fresh and clean. He felt more awake, but far from full of energy. Yawning again, he went back to his bed and locked his legs into his hips, fitted himself into his Inves, then checked himself out in the mirror.

There it was. The face that drove his popularity and that god awful deformity everyone took to be a heart. He used it to his advantage, but it was just another sign of how broken he was. You couldn't even look at his face without seeing something wrong. He sighed, brushed his teeth, wiped his mouth, then called for Peetie, but Peetie was with Liv, so he grunted and made his way to the kitchen. The Pad was miles away; this was home, the haven of the Cantus world, and far too plush for Trib's taste.

Opening the insanely expensive refrigerator—if it was that pricey, why didn't it open for him?—he fetched a prepackaged meal. Their chef kept them around just for Trib, but made his displeasure at Trib not being around for meals well known. Whatever. It was just food. He kicked the refrigerator door closed as he pulled out a bottle of juice. It was no particular brand—they had a chef, after all. It was some specially mixed conglomeration of crap designed to keep him healthy and give him energy. The green slop tasted less like juice and more like old split pea soup. Trib was hungry, so what did he care what it tasted like?

Sitting down on a tall stool positioned next to the marble counter which had a view of their backyard, a small enclosed space with a fish pool and water fountain surrounded by fake grass and a small table with seats for four, Trib unwrapped the container. A ham sandwich with no crust cut into four bite-sized pieces, some sliced oranges, and celery pre-filled with either peanut butter or cream cheese. It was his favorite meal, but today it just made him feel like a kid with a prepackaged school lunch. He sighed, grabbed a slice of the sandwich, and tossed it into his mouth. He noted his perfect fingers as the sandwich went down and groaned inside.

They weren't even his fingers. Yes, he owned them, but they weren't his. Trib was half robot. He was a triplet, born without arms and legs, the runt of the litter. There just hadn't been enough space in the womb. If the gods hadn't thought that enough punishment, he'd been born 97.5% likely to be bipolar. There was other stuff wrong with him, but he didn't care.

He grabbed two slippery orange slices and put them in his mouth, chewing down on the delicious, juicy bits.

It hadn't been all bad. He'd been born with the ability to wield three of the nine vapors. Ementhium, Tarium, and Tituerium. He could basically control the elements, use tokens (like his inheritance medallion), and avatars (like Peetie). He had to admit that being a Trinnie made him kind of cool. Most people were born without any abilities and those who did have an ability usually only had one. Having three was insane.

Trib reached out and eased a little vapor over a celery slice. The peanut butter started steaming. He grinned, then picked it up and crunched it down. Warm peanut butter was always better.

He finished his meal, staring thoughtlessly at the back porch, then grabbed his Mæssan and rotated it to form a motorbike. The Mæssan broadcast an image of the bike, then Trib pumped a little vapor into it and the bike took physical form. Hopping on, he funneled vapor into the bike straight from his suit and took off, running over the ivy wall and up into the horizon, leaving a bright teal trail behind him. His parents would be upset, but the ivy would grow back. That's why they had gardeners, right?

He coasted along the skies and through Myeinth's glowing streets until he got to the school. School was a story all on its own. Yes, he'd gone. He'd graduated from basic and gone on to core, but school wasn't for him. Not when he was in it, and not now. He'd ended up in too many fights and kicked out of too many classes. It wasn't his fault he was who he was, but the adults seemed to think so. All but one. Coach Xius. Coach was tough on Trib, but he was also understanding. He was bipolar too and had fought his own battles. Coach Xius was the only adult Trib felt any kind of connection with.

Trib hopped off his bike and extended his hand, pumping a little Ementhium vapor into the bike and causing it to vaporize. He strutted up to the gym where Coach Xius was inside yelling at some kids. Trib grinned impishly and waited until Coach saw him, then flicked his head up to indicate that he wanted to talk. About twenty minutes later, Coach Xius came over.

Coach wasn't too old. Only in his forties or something, but a little more weathered than most. He was buff, not overly built, with a little paunch, but not enough to slow him down. His short brown hair swirled up into the air like the wisp of a flame, and he had an inviting, comforting smile.

"Hey, son. Good to see you. Need something?"

"Yeah. I want to catch a Vapor. A transformer."

Coach laughed and shook his head. "I'd tell you not to, but we both know that's not going to happen. It's going to come down to practice, son. Practice and your skills. They're not easy to catch."

"How do I practice?"

"It's called on-the-job training. There's no gym where you practice catching a Vapor. Sometimes you have to learn on your feet. Now, keep in mind that you're going to fail. It happens. Don't let it stop you." He winked as he said the last part. "But I wouldn't stream your first attempt."

"Got any tips I can use if I am going to stream it?"

Coach shook his head, smiling. "You always did jump in headfirst."

Trib shrugged.

"Yeah. First, be ready to run. Vapors don't have speed to them until they're captured, but if you wait too long, they'll get you."

Trib nodded.

"Second...No, follow me for the second," Coach said and waved Trib toward his office.

The simple office was a clean, but worn in, coach's office with trophies lining a series of glass cabinets, the typical lightly used dark metal desk, and a black pleather couch with orange neon stitching. A visisheet lay powered down on the desk and a basket of balls was off in one corner while a cat curled up in its bed in another.

Trib admired the trophies with his name displayed as he hopped over the arm of the couch and plopped down.

Coach Xius circled his desk and sat, then opened a drawer and lifted out a medallion. A dark purple that was almost black, the medallion glistened in the bright lights of the office. The refracted light exposed unintelligible writing on the surface. Coach slid the medallion across his desk.

"I'm loaning you this. I used it when I caught my Vapor."

"You have a Vapor?" Trib said as he stretched to grab the medallion. He held it up in front of him, studying the mysterious writing.

Coach nodded to the small, white fluff ball of a cat. "Not everything is what you think. Keep that quiet, if you don't mind."

Trib bobbed his head.

"What's this writing? I saw something similar on the Ementhian."

"It's the incantation used when it was created. Alexander Reyes discovered the ancient language of the vapors when he found them. It's how he harnessed them to create the Corporation. It's said that if you can read it, you can use its full power. Since you'll be head of Ementhe Enterprises one day, I imagine you'll learn to read it. The heads of all the corporations know how."

Trib slipped the medallion inside a side pocket of his Inves.

"Do I need to be able to read it to use it at all? Do you know how to read this one?"

"It will work if you just hold it up and fire Tituerium through it."

"How'd you get it?"

"A woman I knew once gave it to me."

"Cool. I didn't know you had a transformer. How'd you catch it? I mean, like, what is different about catching a transformer?"

"It was a long time ago."

"Oh, come on. You're only like what, 45?"

"Forty, but thanks for giving me five years."

Trib laughed. "Still, you have to remember."

"I do. I'm an Innie like you. I was walking with a few friends, a little drunk, but not enough that I didn't recognize a ghost down an alleyway. I parted from my friends and walked towards the ghost. I didn't get a chance to start working vapor—the ghost saw me. As it approached, I panicked and started pouring vapor into a pool in front of me. When the ghost moved over the pool, I jerked the pool up and over the ghost. It caught it off guard and gave me time to grab the medallion. I spoke the word of the old language and fired Tituerium through the medallion, capturing the creature. The rest is history. Quiet history, right?"

"Yeah. I won't say nothing. So, what's it say?"

Coach leaned back in his chair, thinking about it, but Trib wasn't going to leave without the spell. He donned his innocent, boyish look.

"C'mon, Coach. What if the same thing happens to me? What's there to worry about?"

It worked. Coach leaned forward and whispered the words. Trib had him repeat them twice and committed them to memory.

"Thanks, Coach."

"You'll need more than the words. You'll need a lot of luck."

"Well," Trib said, standing and spinning toward the door. "Wish me luck. Thanks again, Coach."

"Have you thought about coming back to school?"

Trib stopped in his tracks, his innocent look coming back as he turned to look at Coach Xius. "And risk going to Alexandria? Never."

Coach shook his head as Trib left.

VAPOR

Trib actually felt good. It was a nice thing. He'd felt so blah lately that he didn't think he could feel anymore. It happened like that. Sometimes he'd get super down, other times he would just be down for a while. Everyone was like that, right? It didn't matter that he wasn't taking his meds. He could have ups and downs just like normal people. He was a normal person; he was sure he was in the 2.5%. The percentage was just math. Math couldn't tell him who he was, and some doctors who believed in math weren't any more right than the percentage.

He donned a smile, letting that blemish on his face draw the girls to him, and looked into the camera as Ahnd counted down from three. On cue, Trib lit up like he was full of energy—a lot more than he actually had—and played his part.

"Hey, friends! It's Trib, and are you in for a show today. If you thought jumping off my dad's tower was something, well tonight I've got something even better for you. We're going to catch a Vapor. Can't stop the Trib, right? So, are you ready to make a transformer?"

Ahnd cued an eerie ghost sound as he panned around the dark streets crawling far into the city. Vapor oozed across the surface of the dirty streets, lighting it in a ghostly light blue. A car ran through the vapor as the camera followed it, leaving a wispy trail behind it, then Ahnd brought the camera back to Trib.

"Danger. I know, I know. Everyone's told me not to do it, but, hey, I'm Trib. That's just another way of saying I should do it, right? That said, don't try this at home kids...or on the street." At the end, Trib raised a finger just like his father and pointed at the camera, wagging it like some relic of an adult, then grinned, careful to make his heart birthmark smile and leaned into the camera. That should hook them.

"So, here's what we're going to do. We've been tracking vapors and as you can see around here," he said as Ahnd rolled the camera around the street again, this time trailing up buildings where the vapor was thick and ominous, "we've got plenty."

The camera came back to him at just the right distance to catch Trib as he pointed to his right. "And Liv's over there with Peetie. The Vapor is going to meld with Peetie and give us a transformer."

Ahnd pulled the camera back to Trib's face, then

zoomed in. "If you want to see what kind of transformer, you're going to have to stay tuned. How many do we have, Ahnd?"

"Half mill and climbing."

"We're going to set records tonight. Follow me," Trib said with a nod toward the alley.

Trib inched down the alleyway they'd figured for the best shot at a Vapor, hunched like he was sneaking up on it. At the end of the main building, the alleyway gave way to the back alley, which abruptly ended up against the building. Vapor curled up like a living fog, climbing high, then falling over into itself and mixing. It was mostly Ementhium, but some other colors mixed in as well. Nowhere was filled with only one vapor—you could buy any of them at a convenience store and fill your suit, or if you were an Innie, you could just fill up. Here, a thick stream of yellow Tarium snaked through the mist. It was a perfect combination. Ementhium for illusions and Tarium to make the Adori serve as a token to control the Vapor. Trib wanted a little more control than that, so he pushed out some orange Tituerium, the vapor of avatars, to give some power to the vapors and sync it with his own Innie abilities.

The orange liquid vapor slipped into the mix, quickly melding with the swirling magic and curling up into the air. It pierced through the middle of the tempest, then fanned out and gave the mist a ginger hue.

Come on, Trib thought.

As if obeying, the fog began moving unnaturally, its flows pulling in toward the center and taking shape like phantom arms. Between the arms, it thickened, and if one looked closely, a body was forming.

"Damn," Ahnd said.

Trib turned to the camera and bit his lower lip, raising his finger to his mouth, then whipped his head back around to face the apparition. Extending his arms, he pumped Ementhium and Tituerium like a twisted rope, casting it before him. The Ementhium would help solidify the beast, the Tituerium to control it. The vapor rope swirled around, forming a lasso in front of him, then the ghost curled its head and stared directly at Trib with the misty cavities of its own eyes. It howled like a gale force tornado and made the hairs on Trib's neck stand up, a tingle crawling down his spine. He felt a sudden urge to pee but clenched his jaw and kept pumping vapors.

The ghoul leaned back, then huffed and puffed, sucking in vapor and growing as Trib whipped his lasso around. He was going to get this Vapor and own it. He bit his lip, this time not for the cameras but to focus, then lifted the lasso straight up over his head.

The ghost became realer than real, suddenly swinging an arm out with a finger extended and jabbing it into Trib's chest. An iciness pierced deep into his body. It was a intense cold, like when all vapors had been quickly drained from his body. He screamed and heard Ahnd's footsteps approaching.

Collapsing to his knees, his vapor lasso lost its shape, fading into mist and getting consumed by the ungodly beast. Trib grabbed his chest, but his hands went through the being's finger. His jaw dropped open as he lifted his head to face the beast.

"Can't stop the Trib. Vapors, Innie!" Ahnd screamed into Trib's ear.

The world stopped. The ghost stopped. His heart stopped. And Trib wondered if he could be stopped. Had he been stopped? No. No. You can't stop the Trib. It was more than his mantra; it was who he was, and...

Through the thick coldness ransacking his body, he touched his Innie vapors and commanded his body to release them. Ementhian burst from below his torso, and he rose up, the being's finger still in his chest, his eyes glowing with swirls of the colors of his three vapors. It was too soon to say the words and he wasn't holding the medallion, but this was his only chance.

"Voʊ uənt θoʊɛr æsuənt • Voʊ turoʊ θoʊɛr traɪʌs • ətraɪʌs θoʊɛr turoʊ," Trib chanted in the ancient vapor language, the words given to him by Coach Xius.

Trib threw his hands forward and formed a massive pool in the shape of a yin yang with three segments under the beast. He focused on the Ementhium and caused it to swirl, speeding up. He lifted his head to the sky and closed his eyes, feeling his vapor flow through his body, then suddenly he ran out of his natural reserves of vapor, so he called on his suit and pumped everything it had into the pool.

The ghost howled again as the segments of Trib's pool rose into the air. It turned so fast that the vapors were a blur of colors. It was a blade of death for a Vapor, but if...

"Viʃ kɑksɛnæm," the creature hissed.

Trib had no idea what it meant, but the vapors understood. His pool suddenly shot up as if it had exploded like a firework and peppered the ghost's skin with vapor. It thickened, and the ghost took on a blob shape.

"It's Peetie's turn. The ghost agreed," said Coach Xius.

Trib turned around, surprised to see Coach Xius, but Coach pointed at Liv.

"Now, son!" Coach yelled.

"Liv, Peetie!" Trib screamed, holding out his finger.

Peetie took flight, landing on Trib's finger, then Trib turned toward the gelatinous blob and looked at Peetie, a soft tear to his eye, and said, "You know what to do."

Trib flicked Peetie toward the monster, and Peetie flew up into the sky to face the giant cloud. A fine yellow line pierced through the bird and into the Vapor. Peetie exploded at the same time the ghost did. Trib turned around, infuriated, and glared at Coach Xius as the last trail of yellow vapor left his fingers.

"What the f—" Trib started to say, but Coach Xius cut him off.

"The medallion. Use it now and think of your transformer."

Trib held up the medallion and closed his eyes, imagining the huge bearded vulture. Vapor hit him hard. He felt a beam of it passing through him and into the medallion, then pass into the exploded parts of the ghost, enveloping Peetie's remains.

The vapor stream stopped and Trib fell limp, smacking his knees against the cement as he went unconscious and toppled over.

"Trib!" he heard Liv scream.

MY OWN MAN

"Have you ever felt like you went diving headfirst into a cement pool?"

"Ha! No," Ahnd said. "Not as dumb as you."

"Yeah, well, I am."

"You should think about how it makes the rest of us feel. I have been worr...Oh, nevermind. You'll never... Ugh! I can't say anything. I just can't. You're you. That's all there is to it. Just know that some of us care, Trib. Don't get yourself killed," Liv said, getting out of her recliner to give him a hug.

Trib winced and squeezed his head, then felt Peetie land on his shoulder and peck at his wrist. Liv could be so difficult to understand, but she cared. Trib smiled at the tirade and suffered the pain of reaching down and hugging her.

"I need something for my head," he said.

She ran off and returned with a couple of pills and a

glass of water. He downed them and peeked at the vapor meters on his wrist pad. He had some Seignium, so he pointed at himself and gave him a dose of it. That should make the pills work faster.

"Thanks. Show me what I missed," he said as his headache began to dissolve.

"Was cool. Not much," Ahnd said, then aimed his recorder at the wall, forcing the video to replay in two dimensions against the Pad's light walls.

What Trib had felt was a massive hit of Tituerium vapor coming from Coach Xius. It pierced through him and into the debris, or whatever, of the ghost and Peetie. The silhouette of a bearded vulture, wings spread open, appeared in the mist, then solidified. It screeched like the ghostly apparition had, then coasted down to the ground as it folded up and landed in the form of Peetie, laying limp.

Ahnd and Liv had hefted Trib onto a Mæssan car and taken him home.

"What about the stream? How many did we get?"

Ahnd snickered, bobbing his head. "Waiting to ask."

"Oh, just tell him. You made almost three million live. Views are at ten and still climbing. You're the number one stream this year."

Trib leaned forward and regretted it with every muscle, bone, and fiber in his body. She'd given him something just for the headache. He should have been more specific. He collapsed backward, causing Peetie to flutter. "Oh, damn. That hurts. Number one? Setting records? Yeah. Can't stop the Trib."

"I'd say you're pretty well stopped for a while. You look like crap. You almost died. And did I say you look like crap?" Liv said.

"Yeah," Trib said, rubbing his eyes. "A couple times."

"Yeah, bro. Lay off a bit. Ain't hurting to relax."

Trib rubbed his eyes, dragging his hands down his tender face, and yawned, then opened his eyes wide and looked to his left. "It worked though? That's what we saw?"

"Not messing with Peetie," Ahnd said with a snicker.

Peetie agreed, pecking him solidly on his already roughed up nose.

Jankus popped up and came to life. "Three suited visitors have arrived."

They looked at each other, but Trib pursed his lips. There was only one person who would bother them here.

"Let them in," he said.

Ahnd rolled his eyes as Jankus opened the door and three men in suits with boring faces entered.

"Tribinius, you need to come with us," Pej said.

"Can't you see he's in no condition to move?" Liv said.

"Yeah, what she said," Trib said with a moan as he turned to see the guards. "Can't he just be happy I'm hurt?"

The men started for Trib and Peetie squawked, flapping his wings threateningly.

"We aren't asking, Tribinius. Your father wants to see you."

A guard came around Pej and grabbed Trib by the arm. Trib yelped, wincing from the pain as he jerked his mechanical arm back.

Peetie unfolded, suddenly growing ten times his size, his body giving way to a much larger bird with a golden feathered body and white wings laced in black, his beak curving over in a sharp hook. He raised his head and let out a shrill squawk, then dashed at the man who'd grabbed Trib.

The man threw his hands up to defend himself, but Peetie swooped in, talons first, and clawed at the man, shredding the arms on his suit. The man had a mechanical arm, but that didn't stop Peetie. Peetie latched a talon into the wiring on the arm and jerked, then lunged forward and pecked at his face, going for the eyes.

"Peetie," Trib yelled.

Peetie pulled back, taking to the air and hovering in place without flapping, flying directly in front of the man's face as Pej pulled out a gun and aimed it at Peetie. It was wickedly insane to see a flying bird not flapping its wings as it studied its prey, but Peetie was a Vapor, a transformer, a byproduct of the real Peetie and vapor, and apparently that meant he could fly without flying.

"Don't shoot," Trib said. "Please. He's just doing what he's supposed to do. Peetie, come."

Peetie spun around as Trib held his arm out, then lighted onto his arm, retaining its vultureness and intimidating presence while Pej holstered his weapon inside his jacket. Trib leaned his head to the side to make space for the enormous bird.

"Tomorrow. Just give me a day to rest, man. I'm hurting bad."

"This won't wait," Pej said, then looked at Ahnd and Liv. "You're as guilty as he is," he said, looking back at Trib. "Someone stole the Ementhian."

"Shit. I'm really in trouble."

"All hell breaks loose trying steal it?" Ahnd said.

"Yeah. That's why they're here," Liv said. She went to her recliner, plopped down and put on her visor, tuning out of the conversation. "Go, Trib. I'll see what I can do," she said.

"Thanks, Liv," Trib said.

Carefully moving only his artificial limbs, Trib tightened his torso and with enough pain to remind of human anatomy class, heaved himself up off the couch. He could do this. He was Tribinius Cantus. Nothing could stop him. Not even his father's wrath.

"Don't carry me," he said as Pej reached out with suggestive arms. "That'll hurt worse."

Ahnd's scowl was enough to put a damper on the situation if it weren't already dire. As it was, he just plopped down in his chair and said, "Here for you, bro."

They walked.

Of all the times his father could put out for a car to drive three blocks, this was the one time when they walked. Trib felt a throbbing all over his body that he did not enjoy by the time they got to the elevator. Stepping in gingerly—because every step was like being punched somewhere different in his body—the men in black followed him. When the door opened to the top floor, he suffered the walk to his father's office. His father was already there waiting in his black chair.

The office was clean. There wasn't even a dust mark where the medallion had been. Whoever had done this had come in, swiped that piece, then made off with it before...Oh. Not only had Trib shown them where it was located, but he showed them the way out. They had jumped off the tower just like he had done.

Trib sighed and eased himself into a chair in front of his father's desk. His father sat with his hands folded on top of his desk expectantly quiet. Trib didn't give in and speak first.

"I can't say that I expected more of you, but I didn't

expect you would help steal your own inheritance."

"I didn't—"

"I'm speaking. You will wait until I am done."

Trib rolled his eyes and stared off in the distance, refusing to give his father the attention he demanded.

"That's better. Now, as I was saying, your inheritance was stolen. This is your fault. I have insulated you against most of your bad decisions, sans that idiot move to catch a Vapor, but you're paying for that now. I will insulate you from this one, too, but I want your word that you'll start taking your future seriously. You've spent too long acting like a movie star and not focusing on the Ementhe Enterprises."

Trib was not in the mood for this garbage. He was aching all over, could care less about Ementhe Enterprises, and just wanted to sleep. What would get his father to shut up? He wanted to go look out over the balcony and see if he saw any clues, but not enough to weather the melee of pain that would accompany the investigation. Someone had seen the Ementhian in his stream and had the resources to follow in his footsteps and steal it. There couldn't be too many people like that who also had a motive. Who was he fooling? He had millions of viewers and lived in a city with tens of millions of people. Everyone would know about it. Where would he even begin?

"Can't you create a new one? Isn't it useless unless

you have the Cantus blood?”

“How did you know that another could be created? Disregard that. Any Innie can use the Ementhian. It is more powerful if we do. Whoever possesses it possesses far more power than you can imagine. We cannot let it be lost.”

“Fine. Don’t insulate me. I don’t need protection,” Trib said, his voice soft and almost lifeless. He was far too drained of energy. He leaned back, massaging the back of his aching neck, then looked his father directly in the eyes. “I’ll find the Ementhian.”

His father snorted. Caran Cantus actually snorted. Trib must have caught him off guard because the CEO of Ementhe Enterprises always measured every action before taking it.

“What makes you think you can find it? I have teams dispatched to recover the Ementhian. We’ll have it by the end of the week. You disappoint me, son. Most people would leap at the opportunities afforded you, yet you scoff at them.”

Trib shrugged, then winced, regretting it, the weight of his arms tugging at muscles which didn’t want to move. He forced himself to stand, squeezing every muscle in his body and hiding his pain.

“You expect me to be like you. I’m my own man, Dad. I thought you would know that by now. I’ll beat your teams and find the Ementhian, and you’ll see that I’m not as pathetic as you think."

"I never said you were pathetic, but I would like to be proven right about you."

"Right?"

"You act like an irresponsible rascal, but I tell people that you'll grow out of it and be one of the best Cantuses to ever run Ementhe Enterprises. I have faith in you, son."

"Then, let me do this."

Caran extended his arms wide open, throwing up his hands. "By all means. Show me what you can do. My people will still do their jobs."

CURING ILLS

"I'm here to see Doctor Muthili," Trib said.

"Please have a seat. He's with a patient right now, but he'll be done in a few minutes," his secretary replied.

Trib took a seat. He had no idea how he was going to get the Ementhian back, but he would find a way. He always found a way. It would be nice if he had a clue how that was going to happen.

He was also tired and not just from the beating he took wrangling the Vapor. He was emotionally spent, dragged down by everyone around him, and done with it. Well, not by everyone around him—not Liv and Ahnd—but it felt that way. He was, however, done with it. He just wanted to rest, recoup, and come back revitalized.

Doctor Muthili opened the door and Trib put on that practiced smile and summoned up the vibrancy of youth.

"Doctor Muthili, you said to come see you in two weeks. Here I am," he said, bubbling with enthusiasm.

"Hello, Tribinius. It is good to see you. Please come in."

Trib waited for his previous patient, an older man with graying hair who looked very sad, to leave, then entered the office and hopped onto the couch.

"Your toxicology report indicates that you're not taking your meds. Something you want to talk about?"

It wasn't working. The drugs gave him away. Trib was trying to mask the truth, but the truth just kept rearing its damn head.

"I've been thinking," Trib said. "And a problem is only a problem if it's a problem. You see, if something is wrong, but it doesn't hurt anything, then it's not a problem. I feel fine. I'm not having ideations. I mean, look at me." Trib threw his hands up as he tossed on his everything-is-perfect smile.

"I see your reasoning," Doctor Muthili started, and Trib's heart sank. If it started with good news, it was going to end with bad news. He just knew it. "However, the analogy does not fit. Most of the time, you do not experience mood swings. It doesn't feel like that's how people see you, but it is true. Your meds are not for when there are no problems, your meds are for when there is a problem—they help mitigate the magnitude and frequency of your manic and depressive states. You take them when you don't experience problems to help you when they do occur."

Trib wasn't going to win this argument, so he gave up. Taking a deep breath, he said, "You're right, doctor. I'll start taking my meds. I'm sorry."

"I'm glad to hear that, Tribinius. Let's make sure you stay on track. I'll see you in two weeks."

Trib headed out and down to the ground. Instead of returning to the Pad, he headed home and brought up a three-way call with Ahnd and Liv on his Inves.

"Hey guys. I need to rest. I'm going to go home and take a nap. We're going to find the Ementhian."

"Already on it," Liv said.

"Any hits?"

"Not yet, but give me time."

"I know my trixer. You'll do it."

Liv smiled like she enjoyed the compliment.

"You going to be okay?" she asked.

Trib shrugged. "I just feel tired. The last couple of days have taken a lot out of me. Could just be that I'm beat up. Literally."

Liv nodded, her eyebrows furrowed together with concern.

Trib dropped the connection, then started thinking about how to find the Ementhian. Liv would track down any digital footprints. Were there any physical footprints? His father's teams would be working on those, but what else could they have missed?

He yawned as he pulled up, coasting over a tree as he approached the richer part of town. The vibration coupled with his reserved moves ravaged his body as if though he were thrashing his board. He groaned and felt a little foggy headed.

What else was there? What else could they investigate? His mind wasn't in the place for it now, but he did take his win with his dad. They would find a way. They always did. It was Team Trib and they were unstoppable. Now, if only he could keep going.

He coasted into the foyer, vaporized his board, stripped off his prosthetics, pinning them to the wall and using Handyman, then scooted down on the bed.

His mind raced through a chaos of emotions. They had to come in and grab the Ementhian, then jump out of the window. After that, they had to make their getaway, but he knew how hard it was to coast through the sky. They must have landed nearby. Then they would have to have a getaway vehicle and....

COUNCILOR PLOURVALD

Yesveri Plourvald sat upright in his chair as his hologram broadcast into the council room. The Leader stood glowing in light, and his sphere was brighter than usual—an indication he was not pleased.

"Councilors," the Leader's voice boomed. "Let us convene. Councilor Plourvald, you convened this meeting. You may speak."

Yesveri raised his voice. "We are all aware of the loss of the Ementhian. This was due to the reckless behavior of one heir, Tribinius Cantus. Now, there is a danger to our balance. A danger we have not paid enough attention to. The Cantus boy has put us all in jeopardy. He needs to be controlled, and the Ementhian must be found."

"Councilor Cantus?" the Leader said.

"We will find the Ementhian within the week. There is no need to *fear* a *boy*."

"Anyone else?"

"We at Mæssation offer our services to Councilor

Cantus," Illiana Araveyas said a little too eagerly.

To Councilor Plourvald's dismay, the room erupted with Councilors proffering their services.

The Leader raised his hand.

"The restoration of the Ementhian to its rightful owner is the priority of the Council by unanimous consent. All Councilors shall make their services available and deploy whichever resources they can to return the Ementhian.

"You have one week, Councilor Cantus. If the Ementhian is not in your possession by then, I will give greater credence to Councilor Plourvald's assertions regarding your son."

Well, that backfired, Yesveri thought.

The Leader stepped back, and the sphere dimmed. Yesveri pushed a button and ended his broadcast. Back in his secret office, he stood up and sighed, then marched across the floor to his public office. He was in more trouble than he could handle, and needed to figure out a way to end this.

He sat at his desk and rang Caran Cantus.

"What do you want, Plourvald?" Caran said, answering the call.

He wanted this to all go away, but he had exacerbated it. Now he wanted to deescalate, but Cantus wasn't acting amenably.

"I would like to help you with getting the Ementhian back," he said. It was brilliant. Exactly what Yesveri needed. If he was seen helping to recover the Ementhian, then—

"I don't need help. The Ementhian cannot hide from me."

"But Cantus—"

The call dropped.

Plourvald leaned back in his chair and rubbed his forehead. He'd had a brilliant idea, but now it didn't matter. He had failed. No, he just had a hiccup, and now he needed to figure out a better solution.

What's that? he thought.

THANK YOU

Trib rolled over, eyes foggy, brain a mess, body complaining of aches and pains. His face flat, he peered across his pillow and saw the tops of the numbers making up the time. It was enough to figure out it was 2:54. The sun was out and shining through his bedroom window, so that meant PM. He should get up. It was just hard to care, except the memory of his father's derision interjected and ruined his chances of sleeping. He growled into his pillow, then called for Handyman to give him an arm. He worked his other arm into place, grabbed his legs, and popped them in. Standing up, he gave a stretch that made his body complain, but he was done with being laid up and didn't care about the pain. Slipping into his Inves, the world came back to him. He looked at the display on his Inves' right wrist, a stream of messages, and scrolled through them.

Two days? he thought. *I've been out for two days?*

Shaking his head, he started a group call with Ahnd and Liv.

"Hey, sleepyhead," Liv said, her smile as pure and innocent as ever. He liked Liv, and if he ever thought anyone could put up with him, he might date her, but, since that wasn't going to happen, she was a great friend.

"Hey," he answered, rubbing his eyes and yawning, then stretched again. "What did I miss?"

"Not much. We just figured out who stole the Ementhian," she said nonchalantly.

The look on her face was so sickeningly coy that if she had said anything else, he would have ignored her, but now he wanted to hug her.

"Really? You've got to be kidding me. Who was it?"

"Tarah Livings," Ahnd announced without any fanfare or drama.

Trib shook his head and blinked. Tarah Livings? A corporation? Why would another corporation steal a medallion? It didn't make sense. Nobody could lead two corporations. The common law forbid it since Alexander Reyes had ruled the Corporation, the one corporation that had been split to form the nine. What was in it for them? Could they even try extorting him for anything? Maybe they were going to try to force him to marry their daughter? His head swam with confusion, and that last thought gave him shivers.

"What did they say?"

"No one knows we've figured it out. We've been waiting for you, sleepyhead."

Trib rubbed his head. This was something and a half to wake up to. Now that they had figured out who did it, he needed to come up with a plan.

"It's safe now. No one will ever suspect us. Right? I don't want to get in trouble."

Why did he hear that male voice in his head so frequently now? It was like he was listening in on the thief's thoughts. No, his spoken words. Who was he talking to?

"I'll tell you what. I need to go see someone, then we'll meet up at the Pad later. We can make a plan then."

"Someone?" Liv said. Did he detect a hint of jealousy in her voice?

"Coach Xius," he said.

Liv looked surprised, a little too pleasantly, but Trib didn't know what to make of it. Sometimes, he could swear she had the hots for him. He shrugged it off, then killed the connection, walked out on his balcony and grabbed his Mæssan, dialing in a motorbike and pumping some vapor...No, he tried to pump some vapor, but he was drained. Suit and body. Catching that Vapor and the ride home had taken everything he had. He went back inside and changed into a new suit. It was an Inves 500 that held half as much vapor as his Inves 1000, but it would get him where he was going. Suit on, he grabbed the Coach Xius medallion, pocketed it, then was on his way to see Coach.

Hopping off his motorbike, he vaporized it and jogged toward the gym. Trib's timing was poor. Coach had just started a class. He climbed up into the bleachers and watched. Watched and thought.

What had brought Coach Xius to the alleyway that night? How did he know where Trib would be? Why did he think Trib needed help? There were lots of answers, most of them obvious, but Trib had to ask and, more importantly, thank Coach for being there. If he hadn't been there, things would have gone as badly as Coach had warned.

The class ended and Coach approached Trib with a smile, shaking his head.

"Trib. Good to see you. That was a tough night. I'm glad you're doing well. Let's go to my office."

Trib nodded and followed, easing into a seat on the worn couch as Coach Xius sat at his desk. He was careful not to let Coach see him straining against sore muscles. Peetie nuzzled up against Trib's neck as Coach Xius leaned forward.

"We have a lot to talk about. Where would you like to start?"

"I didn't think...Why were you there? How did you

know? I mean, thank you."

Coach laughed, donning a big, friendly smile.

"You don't think I know you, son? You're going to set your sights high, and you're going to get there. The problem is when your aim reaches dangerous heights. A Vapor is dangerous. Trying to make a transformer is even more dangerous. I thought you might need a hand." He shrugged. "Turns out I was right. You're welcome."

"But how did you know where I would be?"

"You don't have to be sixteen to watch your show, son."

Trib blushed. Yes, some answers were obvious.

"What did the Vapor say when I chanted those words you gave me?"

"'I agree.'"

"I see. Well, I could have called and said thanks, but after the risk you took, it seemed better to tell you in person. I don't really have anything else to say."

"Tell me about the Ementhian."

"We think we know who took it—Tarah Livings. I'm going to get it back and show my dad that I'm not just some superstar stream boy."

"I see. You're going to rob the corporation who robbed you? And, I'm guessing, broadcast it while you do?"

"I hadn't put it in words yet, but, yeah, I guess."

"Consider letting the authorities in on it. Just gather the evidence and let them do their jobs. It's safer that way."

Trib shook his head. "The Ementhian is mine. It's my responsibility and my inheritance. I'm going to get it back from whoever stole it."

Coach sighed. "Speaking of medallions. There's another reason you came to see me in person. Let's not forget about mine," he said, holding out his hand.

Trib fished the medallion out of his pocket and returned it. Coach put it back in his desk.

"I can't stop you," he said with a smirk, "so I'll just give you a bit of advice. The Ementhian can't be stolen. Yes, it can be taken, but it knows its owner. Wherever it is, it is yours. There's no rush to get it back. When the time comes, it'll be in the right hands."

Why did Coach sound so confident? What did he know about the Ementhian? Was there some common knowledge Trib hadn't been let in on? Trib shrugged it off and stood.

"Thanks, Coach. I'm not sure how you know this stuff, but it's going to be in my hands before the time comes."

Trib thought about that for a moment, then laughed. "You know what I mean. I just said it wrong. When I asked my dad about making a duplicate, he said the original has more power than I can imagine. You seem to know a lot. Do you know what he meant?"

Coach shrugged. "You can't make an exact duplicate. All the medallions were made together, and just like it knows you, it knows its sisters. You would never need to use them all together, but if someone did—someone like Alexander Reyes—then there would be no substitute for the original. I'm surprised how much your father knows."

Trib laughed. "I'm surprised how much you know."

Coach smiled.

"Thanks. Your advice means a lot to me," Trib said, reaching out and shaking Coach's hand.

"You're like a son to me. I want to see you go far. Just make sure you don't go too far."

Reflecting, Trib left Coach's office and made his way home. Coach was more like a father than his own father. His own father was like a judge, jury, and executioner, not a parent. He didn't really give advice, just orders, and he never showed real affection for Trib. Rumor had it that it was all because of the New Year's Nightmare of 1137, but Trib was too young to remember that. The only thing he knew about it was that was when he lost his siblings. They had been fraternal triplets, but it made him an only child. Maybe his dad just couldn't bear seeing his siblings in Trib's face. It didn't matter in the long run. His dad just wasn't the kind of dad Trib needed. Coach Xius was much more of a father to Trib.

THE PLAN

If Trib was being honest with himself, he wasn't invested in this mission. All he wanted to do was sleep, but he'd been sleeping for days—not all of which had to do with his injuries—and it was time to act, so he was going through the motions, doing what he needed to do, whether he felt like it or not. He leaned back in his recliner, kicked up the footrest, then studied Liv's visual, a vapor model in front of them.

"This is the Tarah Livings building," Liv said, pointing at the three-dimensional view of a towering building. It was similar to Ementhe Enterprises, but shorter and wider, taking up a couple of city blocks. Just like Trib's future domain, Tarah Tower had an inner courtyard, but it was a city block in and of itself. The building was painted in hues of yellow and orange, staying true to its vapor's sun coloring and stood out as a bright pinnacle of light in the center of Tacenteon, a city of light. The hot sun beat down on the glass windows, and the people were dressed in light, airy clothes.

The vapor model expanded in on a top floor, piercing through the glass as only a visualization can and displayed a blurred room. It was too vaporous to make out much detail.

"I don't have a map of the main office, so we can't really peek in, but if they're anything like your father, this is where they're keeping the Ementhian."

"Security?" Ahnd said.

"Light. Make Adoris."

Peetie interrupted with a chirp that made them all snicker.

"I doubt it will be there. They just stole it. That would be too obvious. We need more information. How can we get it?" Trib said.

The building faded away and little vapor spiders appeared in its place.

"I've got that taken care of. I know you said you wanted to make the plan, Trib, but—"

"It's fine, Liv. You're doing great. It's better than what I was thinking."

Truth be told, he hadn't come up with a plan, so he was glad for Liv's help.

"Okay, then. When we arrive, we'll release these spiders on the building. They'll penetrate it for us and listen in. It's ironic, actually. We'll be using Adoris to hack the maker of Adoris."

"I'll secure us a hangout near Tarah Living's tower," Trib said. "We can use that as our base of operations. And Ahnd? We're going to stream this on a delayed stream. Can you delay it by five hours?"

"Yeah."

"Great. Let's pack some bags," Trib said, getting up. "We'll meet at the station in two hours."

Liv looked a little nervous, but not Ahnd. His life had been hard, and this was nothing like the danger he'd been in before. Was there really even that much danger?

At his place, Trib grabbed his newer, depleted suit and tossed it in his bag. Then took his hovercycle to the D&N near the Pad to fill up.

"Give me," he said, looking at their supply of drinks. Vapor came in a variety of flavors for Innies, none of which really tasted that good. He grabbed six bottles each of concentrated vapor, yellow, orange, and blue, a color for each of his natural vapors and set them on the counter. "These."

The clerk noted the excessive selection and raised a brow.

"The Vapor kicked my butt," he said, looking at Peetie. She nodded, packaging up the bottles, then handing them over after he swiped his palm over the payment terminal.

"Looking forward to your next stream. When is it?"

"A day or two," Trib said.

"Any hints?" she said, way too hopefully.

Trib smiled. "Can't stop the Trib. That's the only hint I can give."

She smiled, then rummaged around for a piece of paper. "Will you sign this?"

Trib grinned, letting his heart make hers flutter, and signed the paper, making a little heart for the i's tittle. It made her giddy as all out.

"Anywhere I can change?"

"Yeah. It's not a public area, but for you, sure," she said, then led him to a back bathroom.

Trib changed into his new suit, downing two bottles of each vapor with a sour face. The concentrated liquid was like drinking pure ascorbic acid. He came out feeling like a billion dollars. He was full of vapor, power, energy, and only felt the haziness of his depression. Wait, was he depressed? He could just be sad. If he thought about it, he guessed he was one of them, but right now he was doing something and doing something had a way of damping depression. Thanking the clerk with his boyishly cute smile, he headed toward the transport, calling up a contact and making reservations in Tacenteon on his way.

Liv rushed home. Home was where her heart truly lay. A small apartment in the middle class part of town. They didn't have a lot, but her father always made sure they had everything they needed. Her stomach grumbled for goodness; Mama was cooking and the smell wafted down the block.

"Mama, what is that?" Liv asked, barging into the kitchen following a pot of soup's aromas.

Her mother smiled, lifted a spoonful, and blew on it. "What you think?" she said in her broken English. "Good, no?"

Liv blew on the spoon a little more, then eased her lips onto it, slurping up some magical chicken and dumplings. Oh, for the love of everything good in the universe. Really? She was going to miss out on this?

"Perfecto," Liv said. "Mama, I have to go on a trip with Trib and Ahnd. I'll be gone for a few days. Save me some?"

Her mother pursed her lips and shook her head. "Running around with boys, bad. Stay home, good girl. I save some for you," she said and patted Liv's cheek.

"Thanks, mom. You're the best."

Liv leaned in as her mother held the spoon and slurped up the rest of the ladle, savoring the inch-wide, thick noodle that popped into her mouth and wishing she could obey her mother and stay home. The noodles were good enough to keep her father home, too. If only he had been there.

She ran to her room and packed her bag, adding a variety of electrical devices and clothing. She packed enough supplies for a week even though they should only be gone a couple of days (one never knew how long one would really be gone). Bag full, she slung it over her shoulder, kissed her mother on the way out the door, then stopped abruptly as her mother held a bag with soup out for her.

"You eat good," she said with a touching smile.

Liv hopped on a Mæssaned bike and raced to the station.

Ahnd had a home. It was his parents' house, a clean dump. His stepfather kept it clean, but it was in a dumpy part of town. It was brown to remind them that they lived in a shit hole. As if the broken furniture, having the same bed he had as a kid, and the smell of city garbage welcoming him home wasn't enough of a reminder.

Ahnd trudged into his parents' house and snuck into his bedroom.

"Is that you, Ahnd?" his father's husband, Alex, said.

"Getting something."

"You should stay for a bit. Your dad is coming home

with dinner soon."

"Not hungry."

He heard a sigh intended to be heard. "You really should spend more time with family."

"Thanks."

Another audible sigh.

Ignoring Alex, Ahnd closed the door to his room, then went to his closet and placed his palm against the wall, releasing a little Brumenium from his suit. A fake wall slid to the side, and a duffle fell into Ahnd's waiting hands. He slung it over his shoulder. It was all he needed for this trip. He had a feeling about this trip, and it wasn't good.

The hidden wall sealed up and Ahnd tried to sneak back out of his room, but Alex felt the necessity to meet him at the door.

"There you are. Ahnd, really, you know your father and I love you. Why don't you spend more time here at home?"

"Good guy, Alex. Stay that way," Ahnd said, patting Alex on the chest as he pushed past his stepfather.

Ignoring Alex's calls for him, Ahnd burst out of the house and took off for the station.

People scurried through Myeinth Station, bags in hand for long trips, working their way through the checkpoints toward a wall of boarding tubes leading to tracks out of the building. Trib dodged them and looked over the heads of the crowd, searching for Ahnd and Liv.

"I'm here," Liv said from behind Trib. He jumped and spun around, lighting up when he saw her. There was something about her that Trib...no, he couldn't think about that now.

"Hey! Great."

"I'm so excited. We're going to *Tacenteon.* I've never been to another country before."

"You'll love it. Have you seen Ahnd?"

"No, not yet. What's the coolest part about Tacenteon?"

"Um," Trib said, scratching his head. "It's like any city, I guess," he said sheepishly, then abruptly threw up his arms. "Except, it's a city of lights that never sleeps. The whole place captures your imagination and makes you feel like you're in another world."

Liv ate it up, clapping her hands and eyes vibrant.

"And there's Ahnd," Trib said, smiling and turning to Ahnd as he appeared from the crowd.

Ahnd rolled his neck, cracking it as he did. "Yeah. Am here," he said.

Liv smiled and lifted her hand up to Trib's. He transmitted a ticket, then repeated the same with Ahnd.

"I'll see you in Tacenteon."

"To Tacenteon!" Liv yelled, way too full of energy.

They approached the track, each one getting to a
cylinder before the track and lifted their arms to the
meter. It registered their tickets, marked them as used,
then emitted a glowing red Mæssan projection of a sphere
inside the boarding tube. They stepped inside their orbs,
and with a burst of vapor, the orbs solidified into a glass
bubble with propulsion jets on the back. The vehicles
jetted forward and shot out of the station, taking to the
skies.

They flew in parallel, all headed in the same direction,
flying over land, small outlying cities twinkling like stars
against the night sky, then over the ocean, dark, bland
and endless as ever, before zooming through the outskirts
of Tacenteon. They weaved through a few towers, then
approached holes that looked too small, plunging into
them and Tacenteon Station. The spheres came to rest,
then vaporized, and they stepped out of their arrival
tubes and into the station.

CALLING HOME

The Ementhian could not hide from Caran Cantus. It was in his blood. Lineage passed down from Alexander Reyes himself. That was why he had no need to worry about the Ementhian's location. Except for himself and Tribinius, the Ementhian was little more than a vapor magnifying glass and, even then, it was not as strong as pure vapor.

Caran took an elevator reserved for him down past the bottom floor. The door opened to a room filled with teal gold. It glistened, sparkling with the glow of pure vapor. Only Councilors knew such places existed and what they stored.

Before him was a glowing ball, the Source. All Ementhium on Earth came from it and it was funneled into a long glass tube that ran up the center of Ementhe Enterprises.

Caran extended a hand, pointed at the glass tube, and

ejected all the Ementhium in him. It was the watered-down kind he provided to the world, and he was about to fill up on pure Ementhium. Empty, he walked forward, hand extended until he was within an inch of the Source. Pure vapor swirled around his finger as it filled him. The power was as intense as a drug. A thousand times more powerful than the vapor everyone else knew. He threw his head back as the vapor flowed, absorbing every bit he could. His skin began to glow to match the vapor.

Full, he lowered his head and stared at the Source.

"Thank you, my friend."

He took the elevator to the opposite end, the roof. Ementhe Enterprises was a spire, and its roof was small. At the edge, he extended his vibrant hands, palms up, and threw his head back. Ementhium exploded from his hands and into the sky like rays of light, spreading across the sky like a beacon. It thinned and fell from the sky like a fine mist, spreading over all of Myeinth. He was connected with the vapor, sensing everything it touched as it permeated the city, but he could not feel the Ementhian.

It had been taken from Myeinth? How was that possible? Where on Earth could it have gone?

He stopped spreading vapor across Myeinth, returned to the Source, and refilled on pure Ementhium, then, still irritated that the medallion was not in Myeinth, returned to the roof.

"ɪmɪnθiʌn uənt vɛni," Caran chanted, calling for the Ementhian to be seen, then cast a massive burst of vapor into the air.

The vapor skyrocketed into the atmosphere and spread far and wide, raining down across the planet. Again, Caran was in touch with the vapor, sensing everything it sensed, and he felt it. The Ementhian. Far away. Where was that?

He followed the trail of vapor until he understood the distance. The problem with feelings was that they didn't give you locations, but now he knew distance and there was only one city that close to Myeinth. The Ementhian had not gone far.

He exhaled, releasing his connection to the Ementhium and let it dissipate. He gave himself a moment to catch his breath. He wasn't young anymore, and using that much vapor took a lot out of him.

He lifted his Inves and called Pej.

"Prepare a team," he said as a groggy Pej answered.

"Yes, sir. Mission?"

"Tacenteon in the morning. I'm going with you."

TACENTEON

Outside the station, it was obvious that night had little impact on Tacenteon. Light flooded the city. Buildings were lit up on the outside, bright banners broadcasting advertisements, city lights were brighter than usual, and the roads sported glowing neon lights to guide your path. It looked like a city from a video game with vehicles both on the streets and via the airways, their paths lit by massive headlights which boggled the mind—how did they not blind each other?

It took her a minute, but Liv saw the traffic pattern. Every direction was on a different level and the backs of the vehicles had light pollution suppressors. This would take some getting used to. Trib had been to Tacenteon before, but never Liv. Her family stayed with family, and they all stayed in Myeinth. This was a whole new world to her.

Peetie's feathers were in a ruffle and puffed up,

making him look perturbed and cuter than ever, while Trib was, well, Trib. Cute, focused, and a little bit in his own world. Ahnd was typically indifferent with his dark outfit and mirthless look. Liv thought she might look like she'd just found a new playground, mesmerized by the magnificence and magic.

"Mæssan some bikes. It's a trip to where we're going," Trib said.

"Where's that?" Liv asked.

"Our ops center."

Oh, right. She was too caught up in the city. She needed to be more alert. Grabbing her Mæssan disk, she dialed in a hoverbike. Gentler than the boys' massive ego-boosting bikes, it was sleek and agile. She climbed aboard while Trib and Ahnd jumped on theirs, then Trib led the way.

From the station, they moved through a residential district with bright, tall buildings and people everywhere. Did no one sleep? It went on for way too long, with row after row of buildings on the left and smaller shops on her right, then opened up to a small business district. Small as in for small businesses, but the buildings were just as tall as the residences. And they were lit up and full of people, too. This was truly the city that never slept. They continued and Liv became fixated on the towering behemoth near the center of the city. It wasn't as tall as Ementhe Enterprises, but it was much bigger and as bright and colorful as the Adoris it manufactured. From there...

"Yo!" Ahnd yelled, slapping her bike as she almost collided with him.

She hit the brakes as he lifted his hand and came to a screeching halt. "Sorry," she yelled. "It's amazing, isn't it?"

"Yeah. Didn't get hurt. Careful."

She frowned, bowing her head with embarrassment. "I got distracted. That's all. Calm down."

Ahnd sighed under his breath, then threw his leg over his bike and vaporized it.

"It's here, you two. Let's stay focused," Trib said, placing his palm on the reader next to the door. The door opened and a speaker started spewing a bunch of rules. Liv had heard of such places. They were Traveler's Timies, TTs for short. TTs were someone else's house that you rented for a short time, but there were rules to make it so the next person didn't walk into a shit show.

Usually, you had to be twenty-one to rent one, but Trib had money and with it came connections. *Very nice connections*, Liv thought as she entered. Except for being bright as the sun, with barely off-white walls, way too much lighting, and electronics blaring everywhere, it was immaculate and rich. The living room furniture looked more expensive than all the furniture in Liv's house, and it was white, of course. That meant, as the rules reminded her, being careful not to dirty it up. The kitchen had all kinds of pots and pans and dishes, all the upper echelon of Myeinth finery. It was her bedroom that totally let her fall in love all over again. The bed had a bright yellow comforter with a soft floral print and laying on it was like falling into a cloud—it was perfect since she was not one for firm mattresses. The dressers were empty, but all made of fine woods, and there was even a vanity with a brilliant mirror.

All in all, she felt that her Inves covering her dirty, travel-weary body soiled the place just by being in it.

"I'm going to shower," she said.

Did she mention that her bedroom had a shower? And it wasn't even the master bedroom! The shower head and water pressure were like nothing she'd ever felt before. The hot water cascaded onto her skin like a powerful rain washing away all of her dirt, pain, and worries. It massaged her chest, tenderized her neck, and scoured her face, cleaning her pores and bringing her back to life, a life she'd never known she was missing out on. Was this what it was like to live Trib's life?

Toweling off, she slipped into her clean backup Inves, weathered from usage but still in good shape, then primped a bit before the gargantuan mirror. She smiled, appreciating her beauty for a moment, then strutted out to the boys.

Trib seemed to notice. Even Ahnd raised a brow. Yes,

this place was transformative.

She eased into a plush recliner and put on her visor. "You guys ready?"

"Yeah," Trib said.

She pulled up a representation of the city and circled Tarah Tower and the safe house in lighter vapor, then eased some vapor into the air, broadcasting into the vapor and giving her screen a life of its own. She fixed the display in place and took her headset off, setting it on the arm of her recliner.

"This should be pretty easy, except we're a distance from the safe house—ops central. I want to get the spiders going up the building, then retreat. You guys wait here while I do that."

"No," Ahnd said. "Get caught, need backup."

"I'll go too," Trib said.

"No go," Ahnd said. "You're known. Liability. I shadow. Stream's on delay. Needs backup, got her back."

"What happens after that?" Trib asked.

"No way to know. We have to know what the spiders give us before we can make plans," Liv said.

In front of them, the tower spun around, little spiders crawling up its walls to listen in. They didn't need the visual, but seeing the building in relation to the city put everything in perspective. This was a bigger task than any of the three of them had thought.

"Old outfit, Liv," Ahnd said. "Younger looking."

Did he really have to go there? She wanted to be her age, Trib's age. Not like a younger sister to him, but...Oh, she couldn't go there. Not now. He had noticed her though, right? That was good. What was keeping him from making a move?

"Liv?" Trib said.

"Um, yeah?"

"Did you hear Ahnd's question?"

"No, what was it?"

Ahnd sighed. "Mæssan got faster bike?"

"No."

"Take Trib's."

Liv flopped her hand out and caught Trib on the shoulder. "Your Mæssan?"

He handed her the device, then she grabbed an extension cord from her visor and pulled it out, plugging it in. Her screen lit up with menus. She navigated through them, searching for the right option. Yes, it was built for a male, but unsurprisingly, customizable. Why would Trib have anything less? She selected the female version, programmed that to be the default, and unplugged the device.

"Want mine?"

"Huh? No. I'll be fine. Wait. Yes. In case you need me."

"Mine isn't customizable. Might not be comfortable if you're going to go save a damsel in distress," she said, laughing and handing hers over.

"I think that will put *me* in distress."

"Done flirting?" Ahnd chimed in.

Trib and Liv pulled their visors off at the same time and glared at Ahnd, Liv's glare more of a dare and Trib's more about broken trust. So, there was something there. He did like her.

"Got food?" Ahnd said with a snicker.

She was hungry and by his look at her, so was Trib. Wait? Did he think she was going to make food just because she was the girl?

"We could cook," Trib said, reading her mind.

Liv laughed. "None of us have to cook. Thanks to Mama, I have the best chicken noodle soup this side of the planet has ever seen."

"The one with noodles an inch wide and like super thick? With dumplings?" Trib asked, salivating.

Liv grinned and headed to the kitchen. She put the bowls out, then eased a little vapor from her Inves reserves over them to heat the bowls. The scent took her back to her mother's kitchen and gave her a warm, fuzzy feeling.

"Mmm," Ahnd grunted as he grabbed a bowl while Trib circled around and grabbed another.

"Thanks, Mom," Trib said, cutting into a noodle and slurping it up, splattering his pretty little face.

100

THE TACENTEON MISSION

Three helijets took off from the ground at Ementhe Enterprises, Caran Cantus sitting in the lead with Pej. They were fully armed and on a mission, though only Caran knew the mission.

"Details, sir?" Pej said.

"Plourvald has the Ementhian. He's hiding it. We're going to take it back."

"A corporation war, sir?"

Caran sat back, placing his hands on his legs. "That's not my decision. No one takes my medallion."

"Understood, sir."

"Clear the back and give me some privacy," Caran ordered.

Pej signaled the rest of the team to move forward and assigned one to draw a curtain. Crouching down, Caran stepped behind the curtain and turned the dial on his ring counterclockwise. A moment later, it shocked him, then a hologram appeared of the Councilors' room and the

Leader walked out.

"You requested a private meeting," the Leader's voice boomed. "What is on your mind, Councilor Cantus?"

"Plourvald has the Ementhian. I'm invoking my constitutional rights."

"Have you spoken with him and demanded it back?"

"No, Leader. He called me after our last meeting to offer help in getting it back. He had a chance to confess at the time. His behavior speaks for itself."

"Peace is preferred for profit. I trust you will seek peace to ensure profit."

"Yes, Leader."

"Then proceed. Carefully," the Leader said and walked back into the sphere.

Caran pulled the curtain all the way open and returned to the front, taking his seat. He wanted to go in guns blazing and raze Tarah Tower to the ground, but he also understood prudence. A war would mean devastation to the Council. Caran didn't want to be responsible for that.

"You will follow my lead," Caran said into the microphone for the entire team in all three helicopters to hear. "Our mission is to recover the Ementhian at all costs. The Ementhian is located in Tarah Tower."

The guys whistled their surprise at that news.

"We'll arrive in three hours," Caran continued.

"There is to be no loss of life."

Unless I take it, Caran thought. *Plourvald is going to learn not to mess with me.*

Two hours into the flight, Pej said, "Sir, we have reports that Tribinius and friends are in Tacenteon."

That was an interesting twist. What could he make from that? If Tribinius also knew the Ementhian was in Tacenteon, did he know how to reach out to the Ementhian? Caran refused to believe that. He was just a boy. Assuming he did know that Plourvald had the medallion, would he be able to retrieve it? What was his plan?

Caran thought about that a moment and even thought about reaching out to Tribinius, but the boy would never answer his questions directly. What harm could Tribinius do? If Caran wanted to avoid a war and Tribinius stood a chance, then it was best to let the him try. But relying on Tribinius was a very uncertain route to success.

"How long can we stay in the air?" Caran asked Pej.

"Another four hours, sir."

"How long if the wind is in our favor?"

"Six at most."

That gave them three hours of standby time. Caran extended his hand and vapor seeped out of his fingers, crawling to the floor, then snaked across the helijet and through a crack in the door. He released enough to fill the air continuously with vapor and invoked an Ementhium wind to push the helijet forward.

"The wind is in your favor. Position us 30 minutes outside of Tacenteon and get me real-time updates on Tribinius."

"Yes, sir."

The future of the corporations was now in Tribinius' hands. *God help us all*, Caran thought.

SPIDER GIRL

Sleek, slender, sly…she was spider girl. No, that was ridiculous. Creeping up to Tarah Tower—okay, she was walking, but it was how she felt—she snuck around to the backside near the dumpsters and pulled her backpack around like a sleuth ready to unleash a secret on the world, then pulled out a mystery package and unzipped it. Inside was the devious payload: hundreds of little Adori spiders, each reprogrammed to come to life and do her bidding with a touch of Tituerium. They were pretty cute, if you asked her. About half the size of your palm and furry all over. Now, she felt like a kid playing with toys, not some hero ready to unmask a villain. Still, this was her story, so she got back in the mood of things.

She scanned her surroundings. No one, not even Ahnd was within sight. Of course, she was within Ahnd's sight; she just couldn't see him, but, again, *her* story. Now was the perfect time. She activated the machine learning routine by releasing a fine stream of Tituerium vapor from her Inves, then took delight as the devious critters came to life. They flooded out of the little pouch and scurried up the wall, finding their way into every little crevice, each following a complex series of instructions that would result in the spiders being evenly distributed throughout the tower. Nowhere would be beyond her ears.

"What do we have here?"

Liv turned and abruptly stood upright, facing some giant man in a security outfit.

"What was that I just saw?" he said, lifting his brows at the building.

Liv blinked. She hadn't thought of a story or anything to say, and nothing was coming to mind. In fact, her mind was racing faster than a jet through a vacuum. Did jets fly through a vacuum? She'd have to think about that later.

"Carrie, found. Finding little sister?" Ahnd said, rushing up and looking like a concerned older brother.

The behemoth looked at Ahnd and Liv. His face soured as if he didn't believe Ahnd's claim about sharing the same father, then shook his head and reached for the comm button on his Inves.

Ahnd pulled his backpack around and said, "Don't touch, dude. Ain't messing little sis."

Why did he keep calling her little? She was older than

him…Oh, he had said she looked younger in this suit.

Ahnd caught his backpack and jerked something off the edge, then threw it at the guard. It slammed against the ground and exploded in a puff of vapor.

"Two kids!" the guard yelled. "Backup."

Ahnd appeared through the vapor and caught Liv by the arm.

"Don't breathe. Hurry," he said in an exhale, then held his breath.

She grabbed her backpack and ran with him. They hauled it up the hill and around a corner before Ahnd spun around, grabbed his Mæssan, and spawned a motorbike.

She quickly followed suit, then trailed him as he wove through the streets and back across town toward the safe house. Inside, she tossed Trib his Mæssan and shook her head.

"I screwed up. I felt so cool and powerful for a moment, then some guy treated me like a kid."

"Had to," Ahnd said. "Bought me the time to smoke him out."

"Not you. The guard."

"Oh, yeah," he said, plopping down in his chair.

"What was that smoke?"

"Grops."

Grops. Groppen drugs. No wonder she felt a little

lightheaded and he'd said not to breathe. Still, the idea made her shiver. Ahnd had risked drugging her!

"Where'd you get it?"

An awkward silence followed, and Liv realized she wasn't going to get an answer.

"Nice bike," she said to Trib, eyeing his Mæssan disk.

"Thanks. I'm glad you like it."

Was there something about the way he said that, or was it wishful thinking? She needed to stop overthinking this. If it was meant to happen, it would happen. He would man up and make a move, right?

Hopping into her recliner, she donned her visor, then pumped some Ementhium into the air and cast a replica of the Tarah Tower into it. She adjusted her Inves suit to tweak the vapor, and the tower took on a solid form, though it remained floating. Little glowing white dots appeared throughout the tower for each spider. She took her headset off and stood up.

"I added enough Ementhium to keep this going for a week. We should find out what we need in that time."

"How's it work?" Ahnd asked.

"Pour a little Ementhium into a spider," she said, demonstrating. "And you can hear that one."

The spider grew bigger and started pulsing like a speaker. She jumped. She hadn't expected anyone at this time of day. Everyone should have gone home. Then, again, this was the city where someone was working day and night.

"Why hasn't it been returned?" said a smooth, but aged voice.

"Turn it up," Trib said, his eyes growing wide as he stepped in closer to the spider. "That's Yesveri."

Liv reached up and added some vapor to the spider, increasing its volume. "Yesveri?"

"Yesveri Plourvald, CEO of Tarah Livings," Ahnd said.

"Husband, I cannot agree with you. It'll make us look guilty."

"Guilt makes you look guilty."

"Possession is nine-tenths of guilt."

"Well, we can't go with your idea."

"Why not? It's how we got it in the first place. Clearly it works."

"Passing a problem onto someone else isn't the way to handle a problem."

There was a sigh, then a door opening.

"Sir, we have a security breach. A young woman was found releasing something a short while ago. Security footage was used to track her identity. Her name is Livia Yasserton, 16, of Myeinth."

"Yes, I know who she is. Tribinius is here. What did they release?"

"Adori spiders with eavesdropping ability."

"So, they can hear us? I see." Yesveri raised his voice and continued. "Mr. Cantus, I don't know how long you've been listening, but I think it's long enough that you'd like to pay us a visit. Please come as my guest and bring Ms. Yasserton and Mr. Mesixia with you."

"He knows our last names?" Ahnd asked. He looked a little more perturbed by that than Liv expected.

"What do we do?" Liv asked.

"We take him up on his offer," Trib said. "We're going to Tarah Tower. Now."

THE EMENTHIAN

Hopping off their bikes and vaporizing them, the trio strutted up to the receptionist's desk.

"I'm—"

"Mr. Cantus. Yes, I know. Mr. Plourvald is waiting for you. Please follow me," a thin woman with almost white hair said. She even had white eyebrows. How old did you have to be to be white instead of gray? It was impossible to tell because she wore enough makeup on her skin to make an Adori look bland, so who knew how many wrinkles she was hiding? She was even odder for not coloring her hair. Maybe she thought it looked good?

Adori of every shape and size filled the reception. It was a colorful arrangement of mechanical vapor pets featuring their newest, the Nessi according to a label, in a larger stuffed form hanging over the receptionist desk. Trib hadn't heard of it, but it looked pretty cool. The Nessi was a great representation of the Loch Ness

Monster from ancient times. Fins and all. The Adori version was a lot more colorful and plushy than the original could have been.

The receptionist stood, pressed her palm on a control panel on a wall behind the Nessi, then the elevator door slid open, and they all stepped in. It was a quiet ride to the top floor, and unlike the elevator Trib took to his father's office, this one opened to a hallway across the building from the CEO. Much of the walk was boredom, but on the inner edge of the building, there were windows showing the courtyard.

From this height, he couldn't see the ground, only a long tube of thick yellow vapor pumping up into a network of tubes at the top. It was reminiscent of Ementhe Enterprises. The concentrated vapor was mined from below and pumped into the building, diluted, and worked into the form needed to produce products. In Tarah Livings' case, Adori, though Ementhe Enterprises produced a much larger array of products. The vapor flowed through tubes onto various floors for different manifestations, creating different Adoris for the masses, all of which ended up on the ground floor for shipping to stores worldwide.

For as much as he knew about the process, it was all magical to him. Science was for the scientists in Alexandria. Trib always thought of vapor as more than science. It just did things that violated the fundamentals he was taught during basic education over half his lifetime ago. It was kind of creepy to think of something half his lifetime ago, but he was almost an adult now and basic education covered just the first eight years of school, so it was that long ago. Still, watching vapor turn into product was pretty amazing, whether science or magic.

"Here we are, lady and gentlemen," the receptionist said.

The door opened and a security guard stood in the way. The tall man had as much muscle as the cauliflower-ear guy had fat. Trib looked up at him and started to speak, but stopped as the guard moved to the side and let them in.

Unlike Trib's father's black, ominous office, the office they entered was made of clear crystal with yellow striations. The owner's chair was white with a marbled yellow leather and a golden Adori dragon hung from above. Sitting on a couch was a very prim woman with perfect posture and her hands in her lap. She looked at them and gave a formal, welcoming nod.

"Please have a seat, children," the older man sitting in the white chair said. Yesveri Plourvald was tall, though not as tall as his security guard, and dressed in a bright yellow suit, one that cost quite a bit of money if Trib had the brand right by the cut on the cuffs and collar.

Trib subconsciously curled his lip at being called a child but entered anyway. He felt like they were in trouble, though they shouldn't be. Who did this guy think he was? I-am-justice central? He had Trib's inheritance—he'd admitted as much. Trib's mind got the better of him and his logic vaporized like a used Mæssan.

"I don't get why you're treating us like this. You stole *my* Ementhian. Give it back, and I *might* not press charges," Trib said, plopping down in a chair, his voice more grating than he anticipated.

Liv and Ahnd took less dramatic seats

"My boy, please. I *invited* you here and *welcomed* you up. What kind of treatment are you talking about?"

He had a point, but Trib wasn't in the headspace for points. He glared at the security guard, staring the straight-faced man directly in the eyes, then looked at Yesveri.

"Please excuse us," Yesveri said to the guard. "Does that make you feel better, son?"

"I think I'll feel better when you stop talking *at* me like I'm a kid."

"Of course, sir. My apologies. Shall we get down to business?"

Sir? Trib didn't really like that either. It made him sound old. Would it be rational to object to that too? He wasn't really feeling rational at the moment. Unable to decide, he dropped the point.

"Sure."

"I'm not certain how much of the story you know, but let me...I mean, do you mind if I tell you the whole story?"

His respect seemed patronizing. Trib locked his jaw and stared forward, feeling a little afraid of what he might say.

"Very well, then. Before Ms. Yasserton took liberties and infiltrated my building—"

"It's Livia, not Ms. Yasserton. And she didn't take liberties. We're all responsible for that."

"I see. Well, before Livia and Ahnd infiltrated my building, I'm assuming at your behest, someone else infiltrated my privacy. I think you can understand why I'm a little, shall we say, disappointed in people's current choice of indiscretions.

"Anyway, the first person to break in left us a gift," he said, opening a desk drawer. As he did, a little brown Brumen vapor puffed up and the Ementhian appeared.

Creative, Trib thought with awe. A crystal desk allows anyone to see inside, but mask it with a Brumen vapor shield and it's like nothing is there.

Yesveri held out the medallion and Trib snatched it up. It immediately sucked Ementhium from Trib. The Ementhium swam within the letters and they started glowing. An old voice, speaking words that sounded like the spell Coach Xius had given him, echoed in his head. He dropped the Ementhian, jumping back in his chair. The medallion clattered on the desk, and Yesveri laughed.

"We were debating how to return it to you, but I think you heard that. The problem was proving our innocence. You see, it is not possible to prove you *didn't* do something. We prove things which happen. So, how could we return it without implicating ourselves?" Yesveri said, grabbing the Ementhian and extending it toward Liv. "You'd better hold this. Looks like old Cantus hasn't seen fit to educate his son yet."

Liv reached for the Ementhian. "Don't take it Liv. That thing is haunted," Trib said.

"It won't affect her the same way it did you," Yesveri said.

Ahnd came forward and took the medallion under Trib's close watch. It didn't come to life like it had for Trib. Trib didn't know what to think. Whatever had just happened, he had his medallion, and he'd beat his father's lackeys to it. That battle was won, but now he was being put into another battle, one he couldn't care less about.

"Prove who did steal it?" he asked, his voice embarrassingly sheepish. "What happened?" he added, staring at the Ementhian.

"My thoughts exactly, my...Tribinius."

"I mean it. Both things."

"Yes, of course you do. First, I cannot answer the question of what happened with the medallion to you.

There are powers in this world you do not understand, and it is your father's job to explain those to you. I suggest you talk to him. Second, we thought of catching the thief as well. Pamela, will you do the honors?"

"Yes, husband," his wife said, standing and grabbing an Adori from the table.

It wasn't one Trib had seen before, but there were so many that his lack of familiarity didn't mean much. This one was an owl with extra eyes. She poured some yellow vapor directly into the Adori from her fingertips, and the little owl came to life, its eyes lighting up and broadcasting a hologram into the room.

"I didn't know Adoris could do that," Trib said.

"There are many things you don't know, son," Yesveri said. "This is the security footage of the night your medallion was deposited here. They took great pains to leave no tracks and knew my security protocols."

"Follow it backwards," Liv said. "At some point, they put on those disguises."

Yesveri nodded and Pamela reversed the playback. The footage glitched as it switched from camera to camera until it got to a Mæssan car's doors opening. The perpetrator got out of the car cloaked. They followed footage from city cameras as the car drove backward through the city, stopping at a Traveler's Timey much like Trib's. The car's doors opened, but no one came out. The doors closed, and the TT's door opened, then shut a few seconds later.

Trib looked at Yesveri. "What does that mean?"

"You do need a lot spelled out for you, don't you? They cloaked their movements with Brumenium. The house was rented under a false name and the payment is untraceable."

"So, we've got nothing," Liv said.

"You have the Ementhian, love. Isn't that what you really wanted?" Pamela said.

"She's right," Trib said. "As much as I'd like to catch whoever did this, the only thing that matters is that I—we—got the Ementhian back."

"There is another matter," Yesveri said.

The three teens looked at him with surprise.

"You came into my city and violated my privacy while planning to rob me. I've been more than forgiving, but my forgiveness goes only so far. This will be the last time we meet in my city. The three of you are never to set foot in Tacenteon again. I have been civil, but that civility will not be extended should you visit again."

Pamela took her seat with a scowl on her face. She clearly did not like the harsh side of her husband.

The door opened and a half dozen security guards as big and beefy as the first stepped in.

"You will now be escorted out of this city. If I see you again, Mr. Cantus, it will be at one of the corporations' events, and no sooner. I assume I have made myself clear. You are dismissed."

Where did this guy think he got off? Trib was about to say something, but Ahnd bumped his shoulder and flashed the Ementhian, so Trib bit his lip. He had what he'd come for.

Inside the vehicle, Ahnd held the Ementhian in his lap. It seemed to call to Trib, but the medallion made Trib nervous. It held so much power, enough to suck it straight out of Trib. What else could that thing do? Where would it stop? What would it do to Trib? Why was it his inheritance if it could kill him? So many questions and no answers. That had to change.

Trib took a deep breath. The Ementhian wasn't the only thing on his mind. Yesveri had changed demeanor so quickly, becoming hostile. Trib supposed he understood where Yesveri was coming from—they had gone in and blackmailed him—but it struck him as out of character. Something wasn't right about the situation.

All that mattered was that he had the Ementhian. He had outdone his father's minions. That should amount for something. He could use that as leverage to get his father to answer questions.

Trib locked his jaw, grinding his teeth.

"What is it?" Liv asked.

"Yesveri," he said. "Seems like he overreacted, doesn't it?"

"Coulda been worse," Ahnd said.

"Yeah. A lot worse," Liv added. "I mean, if he didn't steal the Ementhian and we were accusing him of it...I mean, he's a CEO...and we snooped his building. It could have been much worse."

Trib shrugged. "I don't know. I guess I'm over thinking it."

"You okay?" The look on Liv's face said she was asking if he was having some kind of episode.

"Yeah. I guess," Trib said, sighing.

His attention turned back to the Ementhian. "What do you think it can do?"

Ahnd shrugged.

"It's scary. You couldn't even hold it. What do you think it can do?" Liv said.

Trib wasn't sure, but for the time being, it didn't matter. Trib wouldn't use it. He was, he admitted, a bit scared of the device.

"What do you think your dad will do?" Liv asked.

"I don't know," Trib said, staring at the Ementhian. "We beat his teams and got the Ementhian. He should be happy, but my dad doesn't know how to be happy."

"Do you think you could get him to teach you how to use it?"

"I'm not even sure it can be used. I think it tried to kill me. He should have known it was going to do that. It's like he set me up."

"Um, Trib. That means your dad tried to kill you."

"Yeah. I know. I'm going to get some answers. I don't think this is going to be good."

Liv leaned back, crossing her legs and looking irritated. Ahnd pulled his visisheet out and spread it before him while Trib leaned back, eyes fixated on the Ementhian and mind racing. His dad had tried to kill him. It was almost too much to accept. Wasn't his dad supposed to protect him?

And what did his father and Yesveri mean about there being powers Trib did not understand? It was time to confront his dad, and Trib was ready for some answers. Yesveri and his dad might not have "seen fit" to educate him, but that was about to change.

At the ops center, they collected their things, then headed to the transport station. As they headed back to Ementhe Enterprises, Trib grew more resolute by the moment.

EMENTHIAN POWER

"Reports indicate Tribinius is headed to the transport sir. With the Ementhian," Pej said.

"He's touched it?" Caran said with disbelief.

"We don't have those details, sir, but it appears that he's headed back to Myeinth."

"He'll be coming to see me. These helijets won't be fast enough. Land and we'll take jet cars."

Pej nodded and ordered the automated vehicle to land. Once they were on the ground outside the city, part of the team took positions to protect from wildlife while jet cars Pej spawned jet cars.

"We'll need the wind on our side," Pej said.

Caran grunted and they took off. As they reached coasting altitude, he released pure Ementhium that created a wind tunnel to drive them home.

"What else do you know, Pej?" Caran asked.

"Just got news that Plourvald put the word out that

Tribinius and group are unwelcome in Tacenteon. Other than that, we weren't able to get any news."

That was interesting. If Tribinius was banished from Tacenteon, why did he have the Ementhian. It probably had to do with the boy's brash ways. Caran sighed.

"Have my wife meet me at my office. I want to talk with her about our son."

"Yes, sir."

Oh, Tribinius. What have you done now? You can't even succeed without failing. This will end up on Council ears and only make things worse. Could you just once do something right?

"I'm here to see my father," Trib said, flanked by Ahnd and Liv.

"He's in a meeting. You'll have to wait," his secretary said. Cheri was a strong woman in every regard, from her stern looks to her powerful demeanor. She was a force to be reckoned with, and at the moment, Trib didn't care.

"I'll be in his office."

"The meeting is in his office."

"Great, then it will be easy to find him."

"I said you'd have to wait."

Trib huffed, then marched past her, placing his hand on the keypad. It buzzed with rejection, and Cheri snickered.

"Liv?"

"Can't we wait?"

"Liv, please?"

"Fine," she said, sighing. She walked up to the pad and entered in the 24 digit passcode, but it buzzed with rejection again. She laughed. "He changed it."

Bad move on his part. That meant she was going to work at it until she cracked it. That's what trixers do.

"If you don't stop, I'll call security."

Liv released some Brumenium from her Inves into the keypad and it lit up with a sequence of glowing lights. She studied them for a moment.

"Security, Tribinius and group are trying to break into the elevator," Cheri said into the comms.

"Not trying," Liv said. "He only changed the last two digits." Her fingers flew over the keypad and the door opened.

"You can't go up there!" Cheri said, turning around as the three of them entered the elevator.

"Can't stop the Trib," Trib said as the door closed.

Liv snickered, her face flush red. "Did you see the look on her face? I don't think I've ever seen her so mad."

Trib laughed. "She only has two looks. Mad and madder. She even scowls at my dad."

The elevator stopped and they disembarked. This wasn't the secret access elevator, so they had to walk around to Caran Cantus' office. This time, walking through a corporation tower, Trib was focused on the tube of vapor pumping up from the ground. The Ementhian had sucked Ementhium out of him like a vampire trying to suck his blood. Would it have killed him? What was his father hiding? He knew that the Ementhium mined from the ground was used to produce all kinds of things—Ementhe Enterprises was the largest of the corporations in terms of productivity, though profits were regulated to keep them as profitable as every other corporation. Ementhium harnessed the power of the elements and Ementhe Enterprises used it to produce everything from cookware to shields to Augmented Interactive Reality glasses to medicines. It was mind boggling to consider the power of vapor, but a device which could harness that power? Suck it away? That was frightening.

Scarier was that it was his inheritance, and he didn't know anything about it. His father must not have felt that he was ready for it, but...

"It's over. The Ementhian is theirs. We're fine, now."

Trib wasn't ready for more thoughts in his head. He wasn't ever ready for them. Was he hearing the thief's thoughts? No, hearing thoughts was impossible unless you were under a Grop influence, and Trib stayed far away from drugs. Now, what was he thinking about? Oh, yes...

Trib had decided that he was ready to learn about his

inheritance. Now. And his father could always reschedule his meeting. What could be more important than the future of the all-to-sacred company?

He pushed his hand on the door pad and received the rejection buzz. He raised his fist to pound on the door, but stopped when Liv said, "AIR."

Trib grinned, then reached into his pocket and extracted a pair of teal glasses. The super reflective lenses glistened in the hallway light. He slipped them on, then reached up to the edges of the glasses and eased Ementhium into them. The glasses came to life, and Trib saw a latticework in front of him. Augmented reality—everything he should have seen with his own eyes visible with a grid laid on top of it. It was interactive, too. That's why they were called Augmented Interactive Reality glasses. He plied the grid work open, forming a tall oval in the door, then shot a burst of Ementhium vapor into the glasses giving them a fraction of a second to transmit the vapor and change reality, then deftly flicked them off and marched through the hole in the door he'd carved.

"You tried to kill me!" Trib yelled at his father.

Trib looked around at the other meeting attendees, but only his father and mother were in the room.

"You could have knocked. I knew you were coming," his father said with a groan.

"Well, it was locked, and I didn't. I thought you had some important meeting that couldn't be interrupted."

"When your mother and I meet, no one is allowed to interrupt. Trib, I know I'm not the best father, that we could be better parents. I'm sorry for that, but I do recognize what's important. That's why we're always there for you."

"Then why did you try to kill me!" Trib demanded. "Ahnd?" he added, jabbing his finger at his father's desk.

Ahnd jerked his backpack around and pulled out the Ementhian, tossing it on the desk.

"I got it back, but not before it tried to kill me."

Trib's mother, Evie Lynn Cantus, rose and stood next to him, wrapping her arm behind Trib's back and pulling him in an attempt to be motherly. She always acted motherly, but it felt forced, like she was holding something back.

"Tribinius, your father would not have killed you. He may feel like killing you for some of the things you do, but he loves you. We're both here for you, son."

Trib slapped his hand down on the Ementhian and it pulled Ementhium directly through his arm from his Innie reserves and into it. How it worked when it wasn't even a real hand was beyond Trib, but this was all inexplicable magic to him anyway. The letters started glowing as the vapor worked its way into the medallion.

"Then tell me what it's doing, or I swear, I'll let it kill me. I've faced death. Death doesn't scare me."

"Evie Lynn, please," Caran said.

Trib's mother reached forward and grabbed the device, but jumped back when Trib yelled, "No," and the device spurt out a burst of Ementhium, knocking Evie Lynn back.

Caran stood up, yelling, "How dare you?" He flipped his hand around and slapped Trib straight across the face. It stung, but Trib didn't move.

"Tell me!" Trib yelled.

"You want to see the power of the Ementhian? Fine." Caran reached out and grabbed the device and Ementhium seeped out of him and into it.

"Stop it, you two!" Evie Lynn yelled. "Please. This is not how you behave."

Suddenly, the vapor around the Ementhian thickened, wrapping around Trib's hands, then arms, growing like a living glove.

"The Ementhian will not kill you, just like it will cannot kill me," Caran said.

The thick vapor tugged at Trib's arms, pulled his hand free of the device, then wrapped his arms around him like he was giving himself a hug. The vapor solidified into a dark, thick leather that not even Trib's mechanical arms could break through.

Caran lifted his hand off the Ementhian, then looked to Evie Lynn. "Please take it," he said, then turned his attention to his son.

"You're not ready. You don't want to be CEO of this corporation. You want to be some hotshot that embarrasses himself on his live stream so that he can get more viewers. You don't know how the world works, and you don't care. You're not sixteen—you act like you're six, a petulant child who wants to demand Daddy's attention. Earn it or get the hell out of my office."

A knife slipped up through Trib's leathery Ementhium bindings, freeing him. Trib pulled his arms around, then checked behind him and thanked Ahnd.

"You don't know love, and you don't know me. Why would I want to follow in your footsteps?"

"Boys, please," Evie Lynn said. "This isn't going to help anything."

"I don't think he can be helped. At least I have meds," Trib said. "Let's go."

The trio exited through the hole in the door, Trib's father speechless while his mother spoke in soft whispers.

CASCADING STORM

"I don't like your father," Liv said in the hallway.

Trib didn't reply. It was true he had his meds, but he wasn't taking them. He was part of the 2.5%. Why did everyone keep pigeonholing him into the bipolar bucket? He only said that because it was snide and would hurt his father. The truth was that he didn't need meds, and he was a better man than his father.

That aside, what did his father mean that the Ementhian wouldn't kill him? It was sucking the vapor literally out of his body. How was that not like trying to kill him? Okay, admittedly, that wouldn't kill him, but what was the medallion going to do with that power? Something was seriously wrong, and his father was hiding something.

Yes, hiding because he didn't think Trib was good enough. Well, he would show his father. Caran Cantus didn't know his son. He thought of Trib as a six-year-old.

Just a kid. He was far from a kid. He was almost an adult and...and...he had his own show. He earned his own money. He...

Trib let out a breath, trying to control his thoughts. They were taking over. They got in the elevator, everyone remaining quiet except his mind. It kept going, demanding his attention, craving obsession.

Was it worth it? Was any of it worth it? Was fighting his father worth it? Sure, he was hiding something, but did it even matter? Maybe his father was right and Trib would never amount to anything.

Except, he did amount to something. He had already done things. He was already well-known and popular.

But none of that mattered. Not really. Those people didn't know him. He was only a figurehead of a person, not a real person that people cared for. Except, maybe, Ahnd and Liv.

A weight crept down on his shoulder, the weight of despair. His eyes unfocused and the world became a blur. His mind numbed and he cast his head down, lost in the emotion, an uncontrolled feeling of hopelessness.

Ahnd bumped him. "Snap out of it, bro. Pops don't matter."

True. His father didn't matter, but that's not what Trib was feeling—thinking—he felt the same about himself. If someone like Caran Cantus didn't matter, how much more so was that true for someone as small as

Tribinius Cantus?

The weight gained mass. Trib felt angry at it—it was his father's doing. He wouldn't be feeling like this if...no, Trib was feeling like this because it was all true. It wasn't his father's fault. The truth was that Trib was useless, as useless as his father. Neither of them mattered.

The elevator opened. How long had it taken to go down? Trib didn't care anymore.

Livia grabbed his hand and donned an affectionate smile. "Come on, Trib. You're more than this. You're more than your father. Don't let it get you down."

Trib stared at her with hollow eyes, unable to take in the words, unable to process them, unable to...care.

"I need some time," he said, his voice melancholy and indifferent.

"Are you going to be okay?" Liv asked.

Trib shrugged. "Take Peetie. I need some time alone."

"No," Liv said forcefully. "You can talk to Peetie. You can tell him what you can't tell us. He can help you."

He supposed she was right. Either way, he didn't have the energy to fight her, so he nodded.

Trib turned and walked away, and as he did, a tear tumbled down his cheek, over his wretched birthmark, and dripped off his face. He felt the decision. He knew the truth. The truth was Tribinius Cantus was worthless.

BITE ME

Trib coasted along the streets of Myeinth on his hoverboard, swerving between people, hopping over benches, oblivious to his surroundings. Cars zoomed through the streets, tempting his melancholy self. Life was not great. It had its ups and downs, but when everything settled, it was more of a downer than anything. None of it really mattered. The people, the cars, the benches, even his ever-present Peetie. In the end, everything led down the same path, a path he was following now.

He came to a leisurely stop in front of the building he'd selected for tonight. Twenty-five stories tall, it was short compared to Ementhe Enterprises, yet taller than most buildings in the city. He vaporized his hoverboard, then walked up the fire escape stairs on the side. It gave him time to think.

What was life about? He just went through the

motions most of the time. Smiling when people expected, putting on a show of things, making money, hanging out with friends, but in the end, it all amounted to nothing. Could anything ever amount to anything or was it all just a dead-end street that everyone ran down because there was nowhere else to run?

Was going somewhere even what life was about? He'd had highs. Pretty extreme highs. He was popular, not that any of them actually knew him. Family didn't matter. They were only there to run the company, make money, and ensure heirs. If he was being honest with himself, life was about spinning your wheels and looking good while you did it. That wasn't for him.

Ten floors. Fifteen more to go.

"What do you think, Peetie? Is it worth it?"

Peetie chirped, pecked him in the neck, then fluffed his wings.

What did that mean? Did it mean anything? Trib sighed, a tear creeping out of one eye like a Judas ratting him out. He was done with this. Done with life. He didn't want to be. He wanted there to be something still out there for him, but if he was being honest, there wasn't. Nothing that mattered.

He thought of disaffected Ahnd. He would be sad, but he would understand. He probably understood better than anyone. He thought of Liv. Did she like him? No, no one could really like him, and if they did, it was because they didn't understand him. Still, she would be hurt. Thinking of her crying made him cry even more.

Hopeless tears splattered his shoes; he accepted them with each footstep—look at all that was lost. He had his show, but that would only last so long. He didn't want to be heir to Ementhe Enterprises. Outside of that, what did life hold for him? He closed his eyes and let the tears stream as he strutted up the last few stairs.

His mind felt as numb as his cheeks felt wet. He walked over to an edge of the building a bit too close for comfort and felt dizziness hit him. He hesitated to take a step back. He'd made up his mind. Everything was going downhill. He'd lose everything soon enough. It was all just a matter of time before nothing really mattered, so how could it matter now?

No, Trib wasn't going to let life destroy him. He'd do it on his own terms in his own way. He took a deep breath, his body quaking with the finality of his decision, then closed his eyes. Was Peetie emitting some kind of white mist? No, and even if he was, it didn't matter.

Trib took a step forward, his eyes still closed and felt the edge of the building with his shoe. He was close. Too close to turn back. He had to move before someone noticed.

Peetie pecked him hard on the neck. Hard enough to draw blood. Trib slapped his neck and yelled, "Ow! What's wron—"

Dizziness overcame him and he slumped, losing control of his body as his mind went dark and he fell over backwards.

Someone was shaking him. He felt drugged, out of it. That person was yelling his name. He recognized the voice. He should open his eyes.

"Tribinius! Tribinius!"

Trib opened his eyes, but the world was blurry. He yawned. That voice. It was familiar. As his vision came back, so did his recognition. It was Liv.

"Tribinius! Wake up!"

Yes, it was Liv. She was crying and shaking him. Where was he? The ground felt gravelly, like a roof or something. A roof. Oh, yeah. How did she find him here?

"I'm okay," he said, his voice grating the back of his throat as if he hadn't had water in a week. "What happened?"

"*I* happened is what. I programmed Peetie to sedate you if you ever tried it again. What were you thinking? How could...No, nevermind. I'm just glad you're okay," Liv said, leaning in and hugging him.

"Got a set. Get that close," he heard Ahnd say. Where was Ahnd? He must be close if Trib could hear him.

Trib tried to move, but his body was sore and resisted responding. Liv leaned back on her legs and he rolled to the side, pushing himself into a sitting position.

"Oh, no you don't. Away from that ledge, you idiot," Liv said.

"Yeah. I guess I am an idiot."

Had he really? Yes, he remembered his thoughts. He still felt down. What had triggered him? "Triggered?" He sighed. Yes, triggered. It meant he was bipolar and that he was going through a depressed state. It meant the doctors were right. It meant he was a number. It meant that he needed his meds. It meant that he was broken.

Tears creeped out again, leaving trails on his cheeks. He didn't want to be broken. Why couldn't he be whole in some way? Why did life hate him so much?

"Now, you listen to me. We don't want you going to the mental hospital again, so we're not going to report you, but I have a supply of your meds, and you're going to start taking them again. How long have you been off?"

"Six weeks. I'm sorry. I just don't want to be broken."

"Oh, Trib. You're not broken. You're just different. You'll see. When you have the meds, you'll feel better. You know that. Now, you let us take care of you."

"What did you mean about Peetie?"

"When you gave him to me before catching the Vapor, I knew you weren't on your meds again. You kept doing stupid things. I programmed him so that if you were ever in a life-threatening situation, he'd drug you with corazepam to knock you out. Thank God you fell backwards."

He should feel betrayed, but she had saved his life. Unfortunately, he didn't really feel appreciative about that now, but he couldn't exactly fault her—it had been necessary and she was right. Instead of belittling her, he sighed.

The two of them helped him to his feet and shuffled him to the elevator. On the ground, Ahnd spawned a Mæssan car and they got in. Trib stared out the window, his eyes a blur to the world around him, and he cried. He didn't know why he was crying. Was it because he'd be caught? He'd failed? Or because he'd tried and lost the battle to his mind? Or because the battle was still being fought and hopelessness filled him? Liv put a hand on his back, but he couldn't bring himself to appreciate her kindness. In fact, it made him cry even more. Why did other people care when he didn't? He knew he would just find another time, another way. He knew it, and he cried. Life was simply not worth it; he was simply not worth it.

COUNCILOR NORTHUND

It was their regular meeting, and Victor Northund was elated. The Cantus' fool child needed to be stopped, and now was Victor's time to shine. He'd already befriended most of the other Councilors as a confidant, and he'd let them think they were using him. The truth was that he was seeding their minds, sowing the threads of a detailed plan, a plan which would ultimately make him the preferred confidant of the Leader. Then, he could make some changes to the status quo.

The Leader had taken his place and called for comments. Victor waited until the chatter lulled, then spoke up loudly.

"We might as well talk about the Vapor in the room," he said. "Tribinius Cantus is a danger."

His plan was working. Those who had been using him grunted in agreement with him. He had swayed them in exactly the direction he wanted them.

"He has no respect for any member of this council,

not even his own father. Councilor Plourvald has already exercised his right to expel him from Tacenteon."

As much as they were in his back pocket, none of them spoke up. The Leader's previous backing of Tribinius made them all hesitate.

"Tribinius Cantus is only a Trinnie. He does not pose a threat to the Council, but his brash behavior will be reined in. I leave that to you, Councilor Cantus. Bring in your son before I shut him down."

Councilor Cantus glared at Victor, but Victor didn't care. The targets were set on Tribinius. Not that Tribinius was a bad guy; the lit light gathers the flies. A little disruption goes a long way toward major change. Tribinius was Victor's little disruption.

FINDING TRIB

"I brought you food," Liv said.

Trib was lying in bed, facing away from her. He didn't move.

"You have to take your meds. That's part of the deal."

He didn't want meds. He didn't want...anything. Well, he wanted to die. For it all to end. No one understood him. No one could understand him. Why wouldn't they just let him die? Everyone died, after all.

"Tribinius, I *will* call your father."

Fine. Call him. No...he didn't want that. They would force him worse than Liv. He lifted his hand and Liv put a little cup in it. He took the meds and handed the cup back to her.

"Are you going to eat? It's been two days."

He wasn't hungry. He felt only sadness and a longing to end it all. Why couldn't she see that? What did food matter? Soon, he would care enough that he'd get out of bed and go die. Properly. He wouldn't take Peetie with him.

"It's here when you're ready, Trib."

Trib wished she hadn't sterilized the house. She'd removed anything he could harm himself with and even stood at the door while he went to the bathroom. He might as well be in a mental hospital. Except...except...He yawned and dozed off, unable to think about the differences, unable to care.

When he woke, Ahnd was standing in the door like an ominous omen, arms folded across his chest. He lifted his chin up, his way of asking what was up. Trib stared at him lifelessly until Ahnd turned away from the door. He came once each day. It was thoughtful, especially for Ahnd, but Trib just didn't want it. Why were they doing this to him? Wasn't life torture enough?

It went on day after day, Liv and Ahnd caring and Trib wishing they wouldn't. Day after day, he was forced to live. Would it ever end? As the days merged into a week and the week grew long, Trib felt slightly hungry. He had snacked a little during the prior week. More because he knew he should and Liv was insistent, but this time he actually felt hungry.

He reached out and snapped an apple slice from the tray and plopped it in his mouth. A few days ago, it had tasted as bland as an unsalted cracker. The slight sweetness made him feel good. The juice slipping down his throat felt invigorating. He grabbed a slice of sandwich. She knew exactly what he liked. Everything she'd served him had been his favorite. He munched down on it and felt the flavors come to life in his mouth.

Finding himself enjoying something, he closed his eyes and cried, but then opened them and continued on. He grabbed another slice of apple and enjoyed it, leaving the plate empty.

"Good," Liv said, surprising him. "You're eating."

Was that a sign of something? He smiled at her but didn't speak. When she left, he shifted his torso and twisted his prosthetic legs to stand and went to the window. He stared. He stared at everything and nothing. Feeling numb and passively interested. Maybe he could talk.

Turning around to go to the living room, he saw Ahnd standing at his door, arms folded across his chest, staring at Trib. He flicked his chin up, and Trib smiled.

"Better, I think. Not me, yet, but better."

"Snap out of it?"

"You don't really snap out of it, Ahnd. It just kind of evaporates like a blinding, heavy mist."

Ahnd shrugged. "So, no?"

"No."

Ahnd jerked his head up in a gesture of solidarity.

"Here for you, bro."

"Oh, he's up," Liv said, joining them. "Don't think you're leaving this room. I know you, Tribinius. You're not ready." She smiled so caringly, then said, "But I'm glad to see you up." She hopped in around Ahnd and ran up to him, giving him a hug and a kiss on the cheek. "It gets better. I promise."

Trib started to cry. Cry because he *did* want it to get better. He *did* want the feelings to go away. The storm was abating, but it still had large fangs dug deep into him. When would it end? It had to end, right?

He started eating again, but his conversations with Liv and Ahnd were abbreviated. He could only handle so much. Usually, he liked it when things were about him, but not like this. Not like this.

One day, he found himself staring through the window, lost in thought. Plans had snuck into his mind. Plans of things to do that didn't involve his death. His mind raced with them. Ideas picked up pace, flooding him with visions of what could be. It was then that he realized that he was living again. It was then he knew he'd left the doldrums behind for now—they always threatened to return—and had come back to the real world. When had that happened? He didn't know, but he knew one thing: it was safe to be Tribinius again.

He got an idea and snuck up to the door, walking softly and peeking out. Ahnd was looking at his upside down visipad and Liv was nowhere to be found. That meant she was in the kitchen. He eased out and snuck up behind Liv, put his arms around her, and lifted her up, giving her a huge, strong hug.

"Thank you. You cared about me when I didn't. I know I'm not a good friend and that I'm impossible to put up with. I appreciate you. Thanks, Liv."

She laughed, then tapped his hands to be set down, spinning around when she was on her feet. She poked him in the chest and lifted her head high. "Anytime, Trib. It'll happen again, and we'll be there for you, won't we, Ahnd?"

"Got your back," Ahnd said. "Say something first? Easier than going across town. Just deck you here and Liv mother you."

Trib laughed and said, "I'll see what I can do."

Liv scowled at Ahnd.

A NEW PURPOSE

"I think we're safe now. It's been a couple of weeks. That was a close one."

Oh, no, you're not, Trib thought at the voice in his head. Whoever it was, he was going to find them. They just didn't know it yet.

"Look. I've had some time to think about it," Trib said, pacing in the living room.

"About what?" Liv asked.

"Who actually stole the Ementhian. I want to find them, and I think I know how."

"Broadcast its location?" Ahnd said with dry flippancy.

"No," Trib answered with an eye roll. "They were careful in Tacenteon, but were they as careful here? Whoever it was had to make a mistake. All we need to do is find one mistake."

"I can get into your father's security," Liv said. "It'll

take some time to sift through it all, though."

"That's a start. What about the city cameras?"

"Easier," she said, snorting.

"Great. You start there. I'll help go over the footage. Ahnd, I've got a task for you."

"Watching videos? Naughty parts?"

"No. Working the streets. Someone may have seen something and won't say anything to the police or my dad's lackeys, but they'll talk to you."

Ahnd grunted. "Good looks?"

"Well, I was thinking about your street charm. If anyone knows the streets, it's you. You basically lived... I'm sorry. I should shut up."

"Nah, bro. Don't worry. Street rat. Shitty parents. I get it. Still say good looks."

"Your good looks it is," Trib said.

"And *your* money," Ahnd said, peeking up from his visisheet.

"Use the show's money and make sure you're paying yourself."

"I do," he said, returning to his visisheet and snickering as he turned the thing sideways. "Wouldn't believe what I buy. Oh, yeah. Package coming. Inves 1000."

"Nice. Finally saved up for it? Good on you, man."

"Profits get nice digs."

"Okay. Any questions? No? Good. We start now."

Ahnd frowned, misted his visisheet with some vapor, and looked a little too longingly at it as it vaporized. Flipping his legs over the arm of his chair, he hopped up and grabbed his backpack, slinging it over his shoulder.

"Mr. Charm on his way."

Trib saluted and laughed. "Be careful. I know, I know. I'm saying it anyway."

Ahnd shook his head and ducked out of the Pad into the night.

Trib turned to Liv. "So, where do we start?"

She lifted her hand and sprayed vapor into the room, filling it with a light blue mist, then tapped her headset and the vapor solidified, forming eight panels, each showing a different stream. She took off her headset, set it on the arm of her chair, then motioned Trib to the center.

"We each face one direction. It's playing at ten times speed. We can watch 40 hours of video every hour. See what you notice."

Boredom is what Trib noticed, and he noticed it quickly.

"Why can't we just start where it was stolen?"

"Because we don't even know what day it was stolen."

"Split the screens in half. They're too tall and out of

proportion. We can watch 80 hours per hour.”

Liv grinned, then reached out and spun her arm around, slicing through the panels as she released more vapor, then did it again, but swiped upward, splitting them vertically.

“Not proportional, but that will give us 160,” she said as the pictures flickered, adjusting to the new paneling.

“That was wicked cool. How’d you do that?”

“I programmed it to detect the number of panels. I wasn’t sure how much we could watch at once.”

A few hours passed by. There were 168 hours in a week, so they had gone through a week’s worth of 16 cameras three times over. How many were there?

“I found it,” Liv said, jabbing Trib in the back with her elbow.

“Show me.”

She waved her hands around the edges of a screen and used vapor to merge it to its neighbors, then repeated it until her entire side of screens was just one screen.

She touched the panel on her Inves, sliding to the left a bit and the video started playing backwards. Trib folded his arms over his chest as the thief lifted the glass case and jumped off the balcony on a hoverboard, just like Trib had done—except the thief was invisible, masked by Brumenium vapor. It happened in reverse order, but except for the door opening, there was no trace.

"Go to every entrance just before that time."

"I did. Nothing shows up. He must have followed someone in."

Trib sighed a little dramatically, trying to think of what other clues the thief could have left.

"Did you follow it forward? Where does the hoverboard end up?"

"Behind the Lucky Lady."

"What do those cameras show?"

Liv laughed. "Nothing. No one sees those cameras. They're off the grid. Protecting their clients, I'm sure."

Trib bit his lip. It felt like he was being stopped. What could he do to flip the tables?

"I guess we have to hope that Ahnd has better luck, unless you've got another trick up your sleeve."

Liv swiped her hand through the air in a wiggling motion that stirred the vapor and destroyed the screens. The mist faded as she shook her head. "Nothing this time. I'm sorry, Trib."

She sounded so sincere. She was a good friend. Better than him. And they were so close together. He could smell her flowery perfume. She had fawned over it one day, so he bought it for her as a surprise. Now it made him feel like he wanted her. No, he did want her. He admitted it to himself. He wanted her so bad but he couldn't. He just couldn't. How could he treat someone so badly as to let them fall in love with him? One day he might want to die, and another he might be so angry that he wanted to kill. No, he loved Liv so much that he wouldn't say the words and destroy her life.

Instead, he took a step back and smiled his precious smile, the one that made his heart tingle girl's skin and winked at her.

"What?" she said, growing a little flush. Did that mean she liked him too, or did his wiles tickle her fancy meaninglessly like the other girls?

He shook his head and frowned, forgetting his flirting.

"You're confusing me," she said.

"Sorry. Um, you like my Mæssan, right?"

"Who wouldn't, dummy? I mean really, Trib. Is there a more expensive one?"

"Two," he said.

"What?"

"I have one, and now you do too."

"I don't understand. Where?"

"I ordered you one a couple of days ago. It'll be here today or tomorrow. You know how shipping goes."

She jumped up and threw her arms around his neck. "Thank you, Trib! I'm so excited!" She kissed his cheek, just below the heart, then dropped off his neck, held her head high and tapped him on the chest.

"I'm going to check. If you ordered it before your bad

time, I'm going to make you take it back. No going away gifts. You don't get to give those kinds of gifts."

Trib bowed his head. "Agreed. It wasn't a going away gift. You really took care of me when a lot of people would just want me to snap out of it. You've been there when I couldn't be there for me. The saying is that you can't stop the Trib, but I'm not what makes me unstoppable. You and Ahnd are. I love you guys."

And that was as close as he was going to get to saying he loved her. Now and forever. Her gentle smile meant she took it the right way, so he sighed with relief just as the door opened and Ahnd stepped in, the two of them facing each other. His Inves was gone and he was in tattered clothes, his bruised face grimy and hair in wicked knots. He looked like he'd been on the streets for months.

"About time. Who said first?" he asked.

They both grew red as their mouths dropped.

STREET RAT

Ahnd cracked his neck after stepping out of the Pad. The scent of the city wasn't in the vapors or from industry byproduct. No, the city was made of people and people were dirty. People above the streets didn't understand what it was like to feel your bones and see food just out of reach, perfectly fine food thrown away by some glutton of the uppity classes. Dignity was a luxury, not a choice. When you were parched and puddles meant drinking or dying while you counted those ever-present ribs, you bowed before the god of the rare rain and thanked them. Kneeling before God saved your body, not your soul.

And the streets were the home of the pack rats, those packs of street rats who stuck together not out of loyalty or friendship, but desperation. On your own, you could scrape by, but a pack could survive. No one thrived. There was a price. Everyone vying for a higher position, more rations, more entertainment, and less work. Stepping on a fellow rat meant little—it meant more rats would work to ease your discomfort.

And that's exactly why Ahnd wasn't fit for this job anymore. He knew comfort, even luxury. With Trib, he had no wants. He was a spoiled rotten tramp now, just like all the uppity classes, from those sweeping the streets to those who owned the streets. No, he was nowhere near ready for this job.

The only thing going for him is that he was still Ahnd Mesixia, and that meant a lot. He had built his name and earned a reputation, one soiled by an accident, but one that garnered him instant respect.

He walked around to the back alley, grabbed the fire stairs and climbed them five stories, then dropped his backpack and his Mæssan disk off. A stern face plastered across his mug, he climbed down the fire stairs and hopped onto the ground. He knew the lay of the land. He always knew the lay of the land, especially around his home. He knew the groups of rats and who lead them. It made it easy to pick out his target. Three blocks down from the Lucky Lady, Vestor's group hung out in an abandoned playground. Abandoned by children, claimed by street rats.

He strutted over and stopped a couple feet away from Vestor. Vestor didn't recognize him. It had been years. Ahnd wasn't ready to rely on his rep.

Flipping his head up, he said, "Need clothes off your back."

Vestor tapped his buddy on the chest and pointed at Ahnd, laughing. "Kid's got a death wish."

"Calling me a kid? Death wish is you."

Vestor balled up his fist and rammed it right into Ahnd's face. Ahnd tumbled backward, falling on his butt. That was a good start, but not enough.

Ahnd swept his foot around and kicked the feet from under Vestor. His buddies tried to catch him, but he fell and landed on his butt hard.

"Get him!" Vestor yelled.

About a dozen boys came at Ahnd, kicking and punching him. When he'd had enough, Ahnd started kicking joints. Knees buckled, kids screamed. He dodged fists, grabbing them and jerking forward, then punching throats. When enough of them were squirming on the ground, he managed to get to his feet—no small challenge when you're already down.

Ahnd held his fists up as other boys stood at the ready, keeping their distance and a little nervous. Then he heard the charge of the gun.

"Clothes off your back? Inves 500 and thousand coin?" Ahnd said, turning to Vestor and holding his head high while lowering his fists.

"You can have Fretty's. No one takes mine."

"Deal," Ahnd said, then stripped right there. The other boys laughed, but he was on a mission, and he didn't want to be doing this all night.

"Strip, Fretty," Vestor said.

"What! No!"

"Do I have to point my gun at you? He did it, and you're going to do it. Now! You can keep your underwear. The suit's mine... And the money. Where's my money, asshole?"

"Already transferred," Ahnd said, rubbing his jaw. It was dislocated. Damn. That hurt even after you fixed it. He put the palms of his hands up against the sides of his face, pressed hard and twisted, popping his jaw back in place.

Vestor turned to look at the Inves 500 and grinned, but that gave Ahnd the chance he needed. Still naked, Ahnd shot forward and disarmed Vestor before he had a chance to look up or for anyone to shout. Four feet was not far enough to be safe from Ahnd. Not by a long shot.

"What the—"

"Relax. Wanted you dead, dead. No guns at me," Ahnd said, weapon hanging from one hand, suit in the other. He held up the suit. "Promised you."

"What's your game, uppity?" he said as he took the Inves.

"Information. Ain't getting looking like million coin."

"I've got information. You got more coin?"

"Not for you. Been in your shoes, worn your clothes, ate your food. Get shit from you. Looking for fair game. Something I gotta fight for. Not a mark."

Fretty held out his clothes as he approached. "Here, asshole," he said.

Ahnd grabbed the fresh change of clothes, slipped into them standing a few feet back from Vestor, then set the gun on the ground and walked away.

"If I see you again, you'll be lucky if I don't shoot you," Vestor said as Ahnd rounded a corner.

He found a school of urchins on the other side of the tower. He went to a garbage can, pushed open the flap, and looked inside. A half full soda and a fourth of a hotdog. It was amazing how much food people wasted. If they only knew hunger.

"Hey. Why are you so fat? Do you eat everything?"

Ahnd wanted to laugh. He was skinny, buff but skinny. He could even count his ribs, but compared to the little runt of about seven years at his feet, Ahnd was obese. He offered the hotdog to the kid. Ahnd was about that kid's age when he first found himself on the streets. The kid's eyes grew wide and he shook his head as he snatched the hot dog and shoved it in his face.

"You ain't gonna be fat for long if you keep giving away your food," he said as he munched.

Ahnd took a sip of the drink, then offered it to the kid to wash down the food.

"You bribing me? Because it's working," the kid said and laughed, snorting obnoxiously.

"Maybe. Know about theft of uppities' stuff?"

"Stuff done being on the news?"

"Yeah."

"All's I can tell you is they didn't come this way. If they did, I would knows. Didn't use the streets either. Probably the roads."

"Yeah. Figures. Prob uppity stealing uppities. Get what they deserve, eh? Wasting food and living large."

The kid shrugged. "I like their food. They can keep feeding me for free."

"Yeah, kid. Got spirit. Live off them living off you."

"Uh huh. Wanna know a secret?"

"Yeah. What you got, little man?"

"I'm a big boy, not little."

"Right. But a man. Said that, right?"

"I suppose so. Anyway, Vestor's going to jail. Like adult jail. They got video." The little boy snickered. "I get better food here than they get in jail."

"Juicy. Nice work."

The boy shrugged. "You shared your food. Makes us friends, but I got to go."

So, south it was. Back to Vestor's territory. It kind of

sucked that Vestor had sent a couple of rats to follow him. They were good, but not good enough to stay under Ahnd's radar. He slipped into an alleyway, then back to his backpack, grabbed it, then down some alleys and snuck up behind his tail.

A quick slip and Ahnd's arm was around one kid's neck with a knife to it.

"Vestor meet me behind Lucky Lady. Make deal. One hour. Thousand coin showing up, ten thousand more."

Ahnd disappeared down an alleyway, then scaled a building to the rooftop and watched the tail run back to the pack. He transferred another thousand coin to Vestor's account, then set a timer on the transfer of ten thousand. He set his backpack down and fetched a few Grops and some razor blades, both of which he tucked away.

An hour later, Vestor and two other kids came strutting up the alleyway.

"Expected more."

Vestor shrugged. "Too close to the Lady. Don't want to irritate the boss. What info do you want?"

"The Ementhian. Stole it?"

"Ha! First, I don't know. Second, that information is worth more than ten thousand."

"Ain't got it, worth zero," Ahnd said and turned to

walk away.

"I have information. I just don't know who took it," Vestor called.

Ahnd turned back around. "Keeping yelling? Better truce on fight, chat like men? Leave the rats."

Vestor scowled but walked forward and stood within reach of Ahnd.

"They came right here, but that's all I know."

Ahnd looked at the security cameras, raised a brow, and looked at Vestor. Vestor just shook his head.

"I don't rank like that. You know the rules, rat. Got to get to the big man for that."

"What's that cost?"

"Twenty-five. That's to pay the guards to let you in. No one sees the old man. Ten more on top of that for my connections."

"Told me guards. Why pay you?"

"Thought we were talking like men? Your word don't mean shit?"

"Me and another going in. Double both payments. What's the time?"

"9:15."

"Check your account. Got ten thousand. Seventy comes when inside."

Vestor shook his head. "Guards want money first. You can pay me after. You've been good on your money."

"Deal."

"When?"

"Will send word."

"Can't believe you came here unarmed. You're that crazy, aren't you?"

"Ahnd Mesixia."

Vestor's dirty face grew visibly pale.

"Haven't seen you in years. You're a legend. Tommy followed you, but he got busted. Beat a guy so bad he ended up in the hospital. He'll be locked up a long time. You were always smarter. Why are you doing this? What does the Ementhian mean to you?"

Ahnd shrugged. He still had a reputation. He had done a lot of things as a kid, many he was not proud of, and he wasn't eager to return to the life Trib had saved him from. Still, sometimes things were remembered too long. He wished he forgot many of them.

He felt bad for Tommy. Tommy was a good friend and had taken Ahnd's place when he left the gangs. At least he had a roof over his head now.

Ahnd fetched his backpack, leaving the Mæssan inside since he didn't have a suit to power it, and headed back to the Pad feeling sore, hungry, thirsty, and too much like he had grown used to feeling as a street rat.

LUCKY LADY

"You're going to a strip club? There has to be another way. Really, can you boys think about something else?" Liv said, more than perturbed at the news.

An amused Ahnd sat in his recliner, freshly showered and newly clothed. His Inves hadn't come yet and he still sported bruises all over his face, but he looked civil again. Trib would have never sent Ahnd out if he'd have known what his friend would do. He felt in some way guilty for the bruises that must have peppered his body. Every time Ahnd moved, Trib could see some tension in his face. But Ahnd was stoic and said nothing, though he continued staring at his visisheet, undoubtedly enjoying girls without ever having to step foot in the Lucky Lady.

"You have ideas, Liv?"

"Well, no. But you're not even old enough to go in there."

"Nothing ain't seen and done. Little fun. Nothing big,"

Ahnd said to Trib's surprise.

"Just remember, you have a mission. You're not there for fun, even a little."

"You sound like my mother again. I thought we had that convo," Trib said, and Peetie rolled his head, nuzzling up against Trib's ear.

Liv rolled her eyes and stormed off to her room in a huff.

"You ready, old man?" Trib asked.

Ahnd shrugged. "Across street. How's it going down?"

"I don't honestly know. I've never been inside. Have you?"

"Yeah. Show ain't shit. Show love, get to backroom. Negotiate there."

"Got it."

Trib was nervous. He was older than Ahnd, but Ahnd was a product of the streets, and Trib lived a sheltered life. He wasn't good with people, and that included girls. Crowds of people weren't any better. He felt like he didn't have any control in a crowd of people, and in Trib's life, he was always in control. Still, he had made up his mind, and he was going to find the true Ementhian thief. This was the only way to do it.

"You sure you don't want an Inves? I have a spare 500."

"Mine's coming. I'm good. Thanks, bro."

"Then, let's do this."

Just down and across the street, they approached the burly guard.

Taking a deep breath, Trib said, "I'm Tri—"

Ahnd cut him off, stepping in front and holding up his ID card. It showed him as underage, but the guard looked at it and nodded Ahnd in. Trib took the hint and presented his ID card, then followed.

The inside of the building was loud. Music, colors, and women. Trib was surprised to see the women dressed until he remembered it was a strip club. To strip, one had to start with clothes, right? Men surrounded a half dozen stages, each with a woman dancing suggestively in the center.

Ahnd tapped him on the shoulder and nodded, the music too loud to speak over. Trib needed to follow Ahnd's lead. They went up to a pole. A woman approached him. She was clothed, but so lightly and tightly that Trib's imagination found it difficult to see the clothes. She held up a card and pointed at it. The card showed various drinks and prices.

Ahnd arched his head around, smiling at the woman, tapped on some drink and then held up two fingers. Trib was already feeling overwhelmed. This was too much for him. People surrounded him, bumping into him without concern. They were loud, and the music blared while red lights and velvety maroon decor boxed him in.

Ahnd bumped him and shook Trib's attention. He breathed in deeply and let it out, trying to get Trib to relax. Yes. Trib needed to relax before things got out of hand. Ahnd whipped his chin toward the nearest dancer, and she went up to Trib. She was tall, curvy, supple, and made Trib's heart flutter with anticipation. He looked down, embarrassed to be in the club, then she reached down and plucked his chin up, giving him the most alluring smile as she cast her eyes at a tip box.

Trib swallowed, uncertain and intimidated. He dumped a thousand on the tip box. She seemed to like that, smiling alluringly as she sauntered up next to him. He dumped another thousand, then Ahnd punched him in the shoulder and motioned for Trib to slow down. Trib nodded.

This was overwhelming. How did people survive in places like this? Wait. He was Tribinius Cantus. *Can't stop the Trib*, he thought, then donned his boyishly cute smile, perking his little heart up. She leaned down and blew a kiss to him with her glistening red lips and melted his self-assurance. Not thinking, Trib said, "How much for a private room?"

She held up all ten fingers, and Trib dumped ten thousand on her tip jar. She grinned and winked at him just as someone put a drink in front of him. He grabbed the drink and downed the whole thing. It was just a shot glass and...Oh, boy...that stung. He shivered and swallowed again, then shivered as the heat ripped up through his throat. His dancer—she was his now—came over and plucked him by the cheek, motioning him toward the hallway as another dancer came to take her place.

Ahnd caught Trib by the arm. "Careful," he mouthed.

Trib bobbed his head rapidly and swallowed. Head down, he followed his seductress into a hallway padded in burgundy to a doorway marked with a seven. Inside the room, it was quiet except for the thumping of music from the main room.

"First time here?" she said.

"That obvious, huh?"

She shrugged. "How old are you?"

"Six—Eighteen."

"Right. So, what are you looking for?"

Trib's mind scrambled. He was looking *at* her. *For?* Oh, yes. He was looking for something. The Ementhian thief.

"Someone stole something from me. I need to find out who it was. Can you help me? It's on your security cameras."

She laughed at him and shook her head. "I can make you feel good about being a man, but I can't help you find your man." She snickered, then looked between his legs.

Trib took a deep breath and bit his lip. "I...I....Um..."

"It's okay, kid. I'm not going to touch you. You can touch me, if you want. Five thousand a hand."

"Um...No. It's okay." Did he just say no to touching her? Yes, he did. He was so nervous he felt like he was about to pee himself.

She shrugged. "Anything else?"

He shook his head.

"Okay. Five thousand for some simple conversation."

Trib nodded and she glanced at the payment device on the side.

He paid her, then let his eyes stroll down her deviously beautiful body, his own body quivering with nervousness. "I think I should go now. Is that okay?"

"Sure. The door's right there. You don't want a lesson?"

Trib ran out and made for the exit door, slipping into the night, totally forgetting about Ahnd.

He ran across the street and burst into the Pad, slamming the door behind him.

Liv came around the corner. "What? Are you okay? Where's Ahnd?"

Trib didn't answer. He tried to gather his wits. He had handled that so poorly. How did he ever think he could just march in there and get what he wanted?

"I blew it," he said.

"I don't need to know what you did," Liv said.

"I mean, I didn't get any information."

"Oh. Where's Ahnd?"

"I left him. Let's hope he does a better job than me."

They waited and waited. Two hours went by, and still no Ahnd. Finally, after two and a half hours, Ahnd strutted in the front door, smiling sublimely.

"Did you get anything?" Trib asked.

Ahnd looked at him with a deadpan face as if he wouldn't tell and was surprised Trib would ask.

"I mean, information."

"Oh. Yeah. Owing 18,500."

"You spent more than me. I'm surprised."

"Fifteen thousand for information. What'd you get?"

"Let's see what you got," Trib said, evading the fact that Ahnd had outperformed him on every metric.

Ahnd shrugged and produced a small disk. "Footage."

Liv took the disk and slipped it into a slot on her headset, then broadcast the recording into a vapor fog.

A guy a little taller than Trib appeared in a black outfit, then pulled off his hood and tossed it into a Mæssan car, high fiving a shorter friend in all black. That person didn't take off his hood, but Trib had what he needed.

"It's Anton Variega," Trib said.

"You know him?"

"He's the heir to Mæssation. I've seen him at

events.”

“Wow. We’re going to Theodosia?” Liv said with excitement.

“No. There’s a party here in a month. I don’t want—”

“I can hear him. He said my name! He knows. What are we going to do now?”

He can hear me? Of course. It’s just a voice in my head. It can hear everything, Trib thought. I’m coming for you, Anton. Whether you can hear me or not.

“You okay, bro?” Ahnd said.

“Huh? Oh, yes. Sorry. What was I saying? I got lost in my thoughts. Oh, the party in a month. That’s when I’ll pin him down.”

Liv looked sad.

“What?”

“Nothing. Well, it is something. We’ve been part of this, and we can’t go to your parties.”

Trib laughed. “Why would you want to be around that crowd? They’re the worst possible crowd. Besides, my father won’t even let me go to them until I accept my inheritance.”

“You’re going to accept your inheritance? Just to catch Anton?”

“No. I’ve had a lot of time to think about my future. My stream is awesome, and I’m keeping that for sure, but it’s not all there is in this world for me. Why can’t I have more? Why can't I do more? I'm always telling myself I can't be stopped, but I've been stopping myself. I'm not going to run Ementhe Enterprises the way my father does, and when I inherit it, he won't be around to judge me. It'll be my way, and I'll make some changes."

Trib took a big breath, then positioned himself to see both of them at once. "And I want you to be my right-hand man and woman."

"I'll talk to my father and tell him that you're going with me to the party, but we're going to have to take you shopping. Ahnd will be easy. I'll get my mother to help you, Liv."

"I'm perfectly fine dressing myself, thank you very much."

"Do you know what the cut of a dress says to those in the upper classes? What the material and brand say about you? It's not about looking pretty. It's about sending a message, and if you get it wrong, they will mock you."

"No. I don't know those things," she said, pouting. "I'll learn, though."

"That's the spirit. We're all going to learn. You in, Ahnd?"

Ahnd shrugged as if he had no choice, and Trib smiled, shaking his head.

Peetie chirped and Trib looked at him, saying,

"You're in, too, Peetie." The bird nuzzled up against him, chirping softly as if it were saying thanks.

"So, what's next?" Liv asked.

"I approach my father. This is going to take a couple of weeks. He'll start teaching me the ropes immediately. I'll catch up with you guys when I can."

"It's been a while since I've been home. I think I'll go home too. What about you, Ahnd?"

"Hot date," he said with a smirk.

Liv rolled her eyes. "Men!"

FORTNIGHT

Scrunched up in a corner of her bed, Liv jotted a journal entry. Tacenteon. Beautiful, majestic Tacenteon. She had traveled to a whole different continent for the first time ever. Oh, how she wanted to travel the world. Maybe she could convince Trib to give her a position in the company where travel was required. It would take her away from him for long periods, but still. It would be worth it.

She finished a sentence, then lifted the pen to her chin, tapping it. That made her snicker. If the boys knew she loved the feel of writing by hand, they wouldn't believe it. She was *the* trixer, everything tech. Something so simple as a pen and paper was beneath her. Yet, for her, it was as sensual as Tacenteon had been intoxicating. Imagine if he had said they were going to Theodosia! That was halfway across the planet between the Indian Ocean and the Mediterranean Sea. Just imagine.

She closed her eyes and dreamed up the city. Buildings which swirled and glistened under the harsh sun. Like pages from a book come to life. A cornucopia of foods and technologies peppering the face of the city with sumptuous scents and vibrant lights. A city streaming with red vapor as if love flowed through its streets.

Speaking of love. What was wrong with Trib? She had saved his life, tended to him, brought him back from the brink...and then he went to the Lucky Lady. He probably didn't do anything, but he would have if he had the chance. Couldn't he see that she cared for him? Look at everything she had done for him.

Was there something wrong with her? Did she have some blemish she hadn't noticed? Was it her personality? Did he not like her because she was a trixer? Trixers were supposed to be boys, but that hadn't stopped her. If Trib didn't let anything stop him, why should she let anything stop her? No, there had to be something else wrong with her.

Clothes? He had talked about what they said about you. That had to be it. She dressed like the people she was—the lower class. Trib couldn't see himself with a girl like her, a girl of her station in life.

A tear dropped onto her notebook.

"Stupid tear," she said and carefully dabbed it up with the edge of her sleeve.

Her sleeve? Yes. She treated it like it was low class,

just like her. Using it for a rag instead of getting up and getting a rag. She never stood a chance with Trib. He was just so much better than her.

She closed her book, burying her face in her pillow, and cried.

Boys. Why were boys so insensitive? Couldn't she just love who she loved? Couldn't Trib love who he loved? Why did class have to get in the way?

Someone sat on her bed and a gentle hand rubbed her back.

"Little girl. Why you cry? Mama's little girl no cry."

Liv turned to look at her mother. She was so comforting just to see. Like a ball of love that needed to wrap you up. Liv pushed herself up and into her mother's arms.

"He...I'm too low class...He can never love me," she whimpered.

Her mother patted her on the back.

Liv was acting like a child. She wasn't a child anymore. She was sixteen. Might as well be an adult. She sniffed and rubbed her eyes, then leaned back.

"Sorry, Mama, but what do I do? How do I make him love me? Can he ever love me?"

"Mama's little girl can't make love. Love comes natural. Don't matter class or money or nothing. Just comes."

"I guess you're right. I don't want to actually *make* him love me. I want it to be his choice, but what if he thinks class and money matter? He was talking about clothes and cuts and fabrics like I was ignorant. I don't know all that stuff, but I'm not dumb."

"He like you?"

She hunched. "I think so."

"Scared. Girls scare boys. Not all. Some. You want the boy?"

Liv blushed and nodded.

"Get him."

"But what if I'm wrong and he doesn't want me? I might lose a friend."

"Love is risk. Scary thing. Take risk and maybe find love. Got to choose yourself. Gonna love him, you take risk."

"Thank you, Mama. What are you cooking?"

She grinned and waved Liv on to the kitchen. Liv hopped up from her bed, wiped her face on her sleeve, then ran to the kitchen.

Trib was going to make her do it. Make her make the first move. "Gonna love him, you take risk." She had to risk it because...she loved him.

Ahnd waited until the other two had left, leaving the Pad empty save him, then opened the door and peeked out. He gave the guard in front of the Lucky Lady a thumb's up and the guard disappeared into the establishment.

Ahnd left the door open and went to his recliner, plopping down. He grabbed his video equipment and headset, linked them together, and waited. With pass-through vision on, he saw the hot babe he'd taken to the back room and a security guard walk in. They closed the door behind them.

"How'd you know you needed to see me?" the woman asked.

"Confidence. Didn't need to be there. Weren't showing off. Training girls."

"Observant. Especially for your age."

"Old people think age. Ain't old, right?"

"A smartass, too. Here's the video," she said, pulling a disk out from between a pair of perfect breasts.

Oh, if she'd have only let him play. Unfortunately for him, he was there to work, not play. Another time.

Ahnd reached out and took the video. "Got a mark?"

The guard flicked his hand out, presenting a picture.

"Take an hour. Gotta make a model, overlay the scene."

"And no one will be able to tell?"

"Seen my work?"

"Well, you do your research, that's for sure. How'd

you know that Vestor was in trouble? That he was worth it to Mr. Kivinston?"

"Keeping your secrets, keeping mine. Three years, can share," Ahnd said with a snort as he worked the picture into a model through his visor.

He had a model close to the mark's body shape, but it needed some tweaking. While it rendered, he played the video, quietly making a copy of it on the internal drive, then edited out Vestor with a little touch of Brumenium. That went faster than the model's creation, but it wasn't much of a difference in time.

"Was this how you got out of it?" the woman asked.

"Huh?"

"I know you're Ahnd Mesixia, and I know what you did."

"Then knowing not to talk. Might mess up video."

She quieted down, and he overlaid the finished model into the video, animating the facial expression and movements using a Trius corporation routine, easing a little Trium into the video to make it as real as any AI.

He rewound the video, zoomed in, then played it forward, checking for any distortion. When he was happy with it, he emitted some Ementhium into the air and broadcast the edited video.

"Nice work," the guard said.

"Not done. Recording shows editing. Make a copy, get

an original. That's evidence."

He popped the disk out of his camera, then handed it over. The woman took it, bouncing her breasts his way and pushing them up with her hands as she slipped the disk between them, putting on a show for him.

"I know a girl about your age. You might like her. Interested?"

"Girls?" Ahnd snickered.

"We'll meet again."

Ahnd smirked and let them see themselves out.

Ahnd hadn't romanced his way to getting the security footage; he'd found the head stripper who happened to be Vestor's mother. It was a simple trade. Information for information and a few coins.

He hopped up off the chair, secured his stuff, then headed home. He wasn't looking forward to home, but he wasn't going to sit around by himself, either. If he were lucky, Alex would be sick. Then, he wouldn't bother Ahnd.

Trib stood on the side of the gym, waiting for Coach Xius, and thinking. Was he making the right choice? That's what it came down to, but that question was made of so many other questions that it boggled his mind. Every big question broke down into a billion smaller questions, and he wasn't sure what the answer to any of them was, so he waited.

"Trib. Seeing you more often, lately. You sure you don't want to come back to school?"

"Actually, Coach, I'm here to talk about my future. Got a few?"

"Sure. Let's walk."

They paced around the track at a slow jog. Others were running laps, too. It felt good, nostalgic to run the track again. It got Trib's blood flowing and cleared his mind to put feet to the dirt. The running didn't take as much out of him as it did others, but it did work out his torso—exertion of any kind got the system going.

"You wanted to talk," Coach said.

"Yeah. Sorry. Was just reminiscing."

Coach smiled and Trib took a breath, pacing himself, but getting enough wind to talk.

"I'm going to bite the bullet and accept my role in Ementhe Enterprises."

"That sounds like something you came to tell me. I got the impression you came here for another reason."

"My life's about to change. That's scary. Coach, am I making the right decision?"

"Depends on why you're making it."

Why was he going to do it? It was more than to get back at Anton, more than giving his friends jobs, and definitely not to please his father.

"I'm a playboy. Sooner or later, I have to grow up."

"What's the rush? You're sixteen, not thirty-six. Why now?"

Trib tried to think about that but drew a blank. Why now? It could wait. The only thing driving him was a decision, a feeling that now was the time to make his move.

"I don't know, Coach."

Coach Xius stopped and Trib came to a stop, too. Coach put his hands on Trib's shoulders, looking him dead in the eyes.

"Listen, son. None of us are going to live forever, so we feel the need to rush to do things. We rush when we're kids because we want to be an adult and we rush when we're adults because we think we're running out of time. Life is like a game. There's a timer driving everyone forward, but what have I always told you? Keep your head in the game, focus on the moment, and keep an eye on the big picture. You're going to be great, Trib, no matter what you decide to do, but don't rush it, son. Make your moves only when you know it's going to get you closer to the win. The way to win the game of life is different for each of us—I can't tell you what it takes for you to win. Some people like a lot of money. Some like a big house. Some go for family. What's your game?"

Trib went to answer, but Coach held up his finger and shook his head.

"That one's for you. Find your game and play it well

and you'll go as far as you did in sports."

Trib nodded and bit his lower lip. He needed to find his game. It was a good thing Coach had shut him up. He would have just said something foolish, and that was something you had to think about.

"If you were me, what would you do?"

"I'm not you. I made my choices in life, and look where they've got me. If I had a chance to rule one of the corporations, embed my name in history, direct the course of human progression, I'd jump on it at any age. I wasn't born into a corporation. You were. That choice is yours to make. If you were you, what would you do?"

"I'm Tribinius Cantus, Coach. Can't stop the Trib. I would set my sights so high that it would make everyone jealous, then leap forward full force."

"Good sport. Know yourself. You knew the answer before you came to see me. Do you see it now?"

He did. He was deciding to be the biggest, best Trib there was. He was going to have the money, the house, the family, *and* the show. He was going to have it all, and no one was going to stop him.

"Thanks, Coach. I see it now. I know why I'm making my choice, and I'm ready to play ball."

"Be careful, Trib. Too many people believe the higher you go, the harder you fall, and they try to make you fall. The bigger you get, the fewer you can trust."

"At least I can trust you, Coach. Thanks."

EMENTHIUM GODS

Trib felt on top of the world. He was fueled with pure adrenaline, an unstoppable, unconquerable god amongst men. And, for once, he knew it. He knew it before it consumed him. He took a small dose of corazepam to calm him and gave himself some time for the medicine to set in. It wasn't enough to sedate him, and definitely not as much as Peetie had dosed him with, but it was enough to take the edge off his godhood.

To help establish his humanity, he made himself food, washed the dishes, made his bed, and started laundry. He actually cleaned up the Pad. Ahnd's Inves 1000 arrived, and he'd set that on the stand, then looked around for something else to do. The problem was that Liv had already done everything. She was the fiber powering his network, a solid, trustworthy agent of perfection. She even put up with him, but how, he didn't understand. Maybe she found him easier to deal with than Ahnd.

Trib snickered at the idea, then grabbed Ahnd's Inves package and hopped on his hoverboard. He slid down the streets, package under one arm while he coasted around corners, dashed past people, hopped on railings, and skated through life. He had a great life, and it was only going to get better. Everything he ever wanted was at his fingertips.

Popping his hoverboard up and vaporizing it, he hopped onto the steps to Ahnd's house and pressed the buzzer. A few moments later, his stepfather answered the door. A warm, pudgy man with a little scraggle to his face and slightly messy brown hair smiled widely, throwing his arms open and giving Trib a hug.

"Tribinius. It's good to see you," he said. "How have you been?"

"Good, Alex. You and John?"

"Couldn't be better. Couldn't be better. Come in. I'm sure Ahnd will be happy to see you."

Ahnd stood behind Alex, rolling his eyes. "Done?" he said.

"Oh, Ahnd. Serious Ahnd. I do wish you would lighten up."

"Thanks for advice." It was then that he noticed the package and lit up with enough excitement to power Ementhe Enterprises for a day. For Ahnd, that meant he smiled. "My Inves. Sweet," he said, reaching out.

Trib handed the package over and they went to Ahnd's room.

"How's it going?" Trib asked as Ahnd started stripping. Most boys his age would be shy about stripping naked in front of someone, especially a male friend, but Ahnd didn't know modesty and wasn't embarrassed about anything.

"Great, now that I've got this," he said, slipping a leg into the suit. "Oh, nice. The inside is softer. They totally make this worth it."

Trib smiled, recalling his first Inves 1000. "Yeah. I love it. They're expensive to fill. You got enough for it?"

Ahnd frowned at the condescension. "Show pays well."

Trib was sorry he asked. "Right. I thought you would, but you didn't see it, did you? There's an extra bag in there. Your first fill is free."

"Oh, didn't know. Nice!"

Trib smiled. They didn't give you your first fill free, but he wasn't going to make Ahnd feel like a charity case. He was worth every penny, and a friend like Ahnd was worth far more than that.

Ahnd began filling the suit and looked up at Trib with concern. "Told him?"

Trib shook his head.

"When?"

"Next."

"Good luck, bro."

"Thanks, but I'm not going to need it. I've got this. My father will think he's won, but he isn't playing the game."

"Game?"

"Oh. Just something Coach told me."

"Whatever game, hope you win."

"Thanks. I'm taking home the trophy," Trib said, then made his way out, saying goodbye to Alex. Where was John? He never seemed to be around. It was no wonder Ahnd didn't have a good relationship with his dad.

Trib opted for the freedom of his hoverboard on the way to Ementhe Enterprises. Strutting into the building, he smiled his trademark perfect smile and nodded to Cheri with almost a bow. The show of deference and respect surprised her.

"How are we today, Mr. Cantus?"

"Remarkably well. Can you tell my father that the heir of Ementhe Enterprises wishes to see him?"

"Oh, the heir, now? I see. I'll usher your message along to him with due haste," she said, keeping up formality with a hint of pleased amusement to her voice.

A few moments later, she said, "Mr. Cantus will see you now, Mr. Cantus."

Trib bowed again with equal performance. "Much

obliged."

Cheri giggled. The woman of brimstone and fire actually acted like a little girl.

Up the elevator and across the building, Trib found himself back at his father's door. Repaired, it opened to his palm print. As the door slid open, Trib smiled at his mother sitting prim and proper on the couch, a proud grin across her face.

"I've asked your mother to join us. You have something to tell us, Tribinius?"

Trib grabbed the chair and slid it to the side so that he could face them both, then sat and leaned back, folding his hands in his lap.

"Mom, Dad. I'm not ready to be the CEO of Ementhe Enterprises. There's a lot to learn and I don't have my priorities straight. I get that, but I think I'm ready to be the heir. I can still be me and live my life. I can still have my stream. But I can also be responsible and take my future seriously. I've told you no before, and that was the right thing to do—I wasn't ready to be the heir. I am now. Can you accept that?"

"Depends," his father said, to his mother's chagrin. "What made you change your mind?"

"I'm not thirteen anymore. I'm almost an adult. I need to start acting like one, and that means thinking about my future. I love my show, but it isn't going to be there forever. I'll get old and boring and no one will want to watch it. No offense.”

“In that case, we accept,” his father said, and his mother gave an approving nod.

“I have one condition,” Trib said to his father, who raised a brow of concern. “Ahnd and Liv are part of the package. I want to bring them on to the team.”

“I always thought you’d marry that girl,” his mother said.

“Mom! I’m not *that* ready to be an adult. She’s one of my best friends, not my girlfriend.”

His mother shrugged.

“But I would like you to take her under your wing. She doesn’t know her way around our kind of people. Make her your protégé and prepare her to be on the team.”

“I can do that,” his mother said.

“Don’t expect me to take Ahnd on,” his father said. “I’ll mentor you. You’re responsible for your friends.”

“Sounds like we have a deal,” Trib said.

“If they don’t cause any trouble.”

“So, how do we start? I mean, like what do I do?”

“Follow me. I’m going to give you a tour.”

“I’ve had a tour.”

“You have not had the heir’s tour.”

“Okay.” Trib stood and put his hands behind his back, waiting for his father.

Caran rose and said, "My dear Evie Lynn, the day I have waited for all my life is here. Your son and I will return."

"Yes, my dear husband."

That was a little cinematic of them. Adults were weird. Trib nodded to his mother and followed his father out to the hallway.

"There are 120 floors of manufacturing to Ementhe Enterprises," his father began. "And another 20 for research. The remaining ten floors are for miscellaneous things like shipping, administration, etc. All of them are powered by Ementhium. This city is built around the only natural supply of Ementhium on Earth, and so is this tower."

Trib thought this was supposed to be a special tour, but he'd heard all of this as a little boy.

"You and I were born with the innate ability to harness Ementhium, a blessing that will be passed down to your children. But we are more than Innies descendant from Alexander Reyes, we are the guardians of Ementhium. That's why the medallion interacted with you. It knows its master. It wasn't trying to kill you. It was bonding with you and offering its services. With it, you can control all the Ementhium on Earth, near or far."

That last part Trib had not heard as a child.

"So, we're like gods of Ementhium?"

"I'm tired of hearing these voices in my head," the female voice said.

So was Trib. Couldn't they at least have any meaning? Maybe they did. No, they couldn't. The moment he started believing the voices in his head were real was the moment he really was crazy.

"We are its master, not its god."

Trib didn't get the difference. "Can we run out of Ementhium?"

In response, his father led Trib to the elevator forbidden to use. Only his father used it. They descended to a floor labeled "E", and the door opened. Inside, a large light blue sphere pulsed, throbbing slowly, like a heartbeat in agony in a room that glowed Ementhium's teal hue.

"This is the source of Ementhium. It never changes size and always outputs the same amount of Ementhium. Its power is limitless."

"What if we used the Ementhian to suck out all the vapor?"

"We are masters of Ementhium. That also means stewards. Would you destroy your home to prove you could, or would you protect it?"

"Protect it. Can I touch it?"

"Reach out, but do not touch it. It will fill you with pure Ementhium vapor."

"What happens if I touch it?"

His father glowered at him, so Trib dropped the question and stepped forward carefully, his hand extended. A swirl of Ementhium vapor curled out and touched his fingers. It coiled around his arm like a snake claiming prey, then pierced into his body, filling Trib with an intense sensation that made his entire body tingle. The Ementhium vapor he bought from the stores was air compared to this. It was like life itself had been injected into him, and he felt intensely powerful.

"That's enough," his father said, and Trib pulled back.

As the vapor unwound from him, he felt a loss, as if a lover had just taken their heart back. He wanted more. To never let go.

"I will prepare your training. Come back in a week," his father said. "And you are never to come down here without me. That elevator works only for me, and I will not look kindly upon your young friend Livia attempting to hack her way in."

"Understood."

Despite what his father said, Trib was a god of Ementhium. He could command it and control it like no one else on Earth (other than his father). No matter how near or far? It was unfathomable. No wonder his father had kept this a secret until Trib was ready. Trib didn't know what to make of it, but with the pure Ementhium coursing through his veins, he felt the urge to do something fantastic. But what?

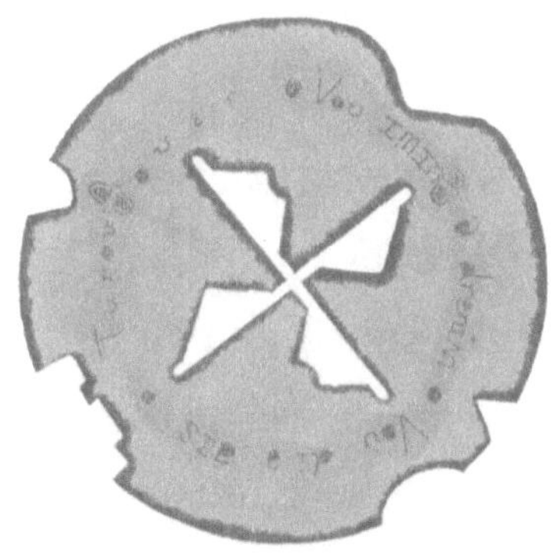

CARAN'S CONTRACT

Councilor Cantus sat as ready as ever. His was a refined house with good, clear lineage and one of the top producers. Everyone benefited under his profitability according to the Contract. It was outdated, but it served its purpose—it guided the basic interactions of all Councilors and corporations. The Contract was the constitution only the Council knew of.

And, today, he was the only member of the Council in the room.

The sphere glowed and the Leader stepped out, basking in the glow.

"Is your son in the fold?"

"Yes. He agreed to his rightful inheritance. I have shown him the Ementhian Source."

"It was premature to show him the Source. He is immature and will not respect it."

"Aren't we all? Were you?"

The sphere glowed brighter, and Caran made note to watch his words.

"For now, I will allow this. He's only a Trinnie."

"Thank you, Leader."

"If he fails this council, you fail."

"He will be great. He will do things none of us have done," Caran said, sounding too much like he was pleading.

"That's the problem, not the promise."

The Leader took a step back and disappeared into the sphere's light.

For a moment, Caran wished he could see the Leader so that he could strangle the man, but sensibility hit him and he sneered at the idea. The Leader was more powerful than Alexander Reyes—there had only been one Leader in over 1100 years, and the Leader was the only person who could wield the tenth vapor. Caran would be dead before he could lift a finger.

At least his son had shown a semblance of sanity for once and accepted his birthright. Caran closed the connection, deciding to watch what idiotic thing Tribinius was about to do while filled with pure Ementhium for the first time.

TRACK DANCE

Trib pulled up a three-way call with Liv and Ahnd.

"Can't talk now, but meet me at the gym. I'll bring your camera, Ahnd. We're going to do a show."

He disconnected the call before either of them had a chance to reply with anything other than looks of shock, then hopped on his hoverboard and stopped by the Pad to pick up Ahnd's camera equipment before heading to the gym. His mind was swimming in possibilities. Being full of pure Ementhium was like nothing else he'd ever felt. A high larger than his biggest manic episode, yet he felt in control, like the power was so real and supreme that he'd reached a plateau and found inner calm. He felt like he could do anything, but, for once, he didn't want to rule the world. He wanted to celebrate it, the source of this magnificence, and share it with everyone.

He coasted along the streets, headed toward the school, and Ahnd caught up with him.

"What's up?"

"Oh, good. You're here. Let's stop here."

They curved around their hoverboards, coming to a stop facing each other. Ahnd was looking good in his new Inves 1000. Trib handed Ahnd his equipment, then Ahnd whipped his camera up.

"Going on?"

"Start on the school in the distance. I'll voice over."

Ahnd aimed the camera at the school, then counted down from three.

"Hi, friends," Trib said. "There she is, but what is she? A core school? Nope, not tonight. Tonight, that's the scene of the biggest party ever. Come meet me at the track…"

Trib tapped Ahnd's shoulder, and Ahnd spun around, directing the camera at Trib. Trib waited for a count of one—the time it would take Ahnd to zoom in on him—smiled, wielding his birthmark heart, then leaned into the camera.

"Can't stop the Trib," he said, and winked.

"Off," Ahnd said.

"Great. Let's go."

"DJ? Lights? Anything?"

"Yeah. Everything but the DJ. Thanks."

Trib sifted through his contact list on his Inves, then nodded. He found the perfect DJ.

"Wanna be famous?" Trib said, calling her hologram up and not giving her a chance to greet him.

"At the track?" a woman with a smoky voice said.

"Yeah. Glad you're watching."

"Only for you. Can't stop the Trib," she said.

"I'll send a car for you."

"I have a car."

"Not like these. You're a rock star, and you're going to show up like one."

"It's retro happy hardcore, not rock," she said, then blew a kiss into the microphone. "I'll be ready."

Trib cut the line and ordered a car to pick her up, then they continued to the school, rounding the building and hopping off their hoverboards in the back toward the track. The gate was locked. That made sense, but Trib hadn't expected it.

"Climb?" Ahnd suggested.

No. Trib didn't need to climb anything. He was flowing in power, the power to harness the elements. It was so strong that he could feel them. He didn't even need his Inves to funnel the energy and direct it; he had complete control over his Ementhium power. Pulling the moisture from the air and stirring the ground, Trib built a stairway out of the dirt and used the moisture to harden it, first saturating it, then drying it rapidly.

"Can't do that, bro."

"What?"

"Use vapor like magic. Glowing blue, something's happened. People gotta think tech."

"Good point, Ahnd. Don't worry. It won't last, but I have enough to power this party. You know how most people and most Inveses can hold up to 1000 reyes of vapor? I can hold 1500."

"How?"

"I don't know how it works, Ahnd. I just know that's what it takes to fill up."

"Cool."

"I'm glowing because I'm full. There's such a thing as pure Ementhium vapor. I'm full of it." Trib stopped leaning in as if he were telling a secret and grew a devious grin. "Now, let's go have some fun."

People were already assembling, having found ways in. Most used Trib's makeshift stairway.

"We have to be ready for when she gets here," Trib said.

"Who?"

"DJ VaporLight."

"The hell? Already famous. Not making famous."

Trib smirked. "We hire her for events all the time."

They climbed up the bleachers to the edge of a wall to give Ahnd a good view of the incoming traffic. He counted down from three, then went live.

"Hundreds of people are here, but the star of the show has yet to arrive."

Timed perfectly, the car came into camera view.

"And here she is...Who will our DJ be tonight?"

The driver got out and opened the passenger door, then extended his hand to help her out.

"It's none other than DJ VaporLight!" Trib raised his voice so high that it almost cracked when he yelled her name, but the crowd erupted in cheers.

Trib tapped Ahnd's shoulder, and Ahnd turned the camera to face Trib. Trib smiled. "In just minutes, we'll go live with DJ VaporLight right here on the track at Ementhe's core school. And that's not the only surprise. I have...upgrades to show you."

As they unpacked DJ VaporLight's set, the crowd doubled, then doubled again.

"Let's get this show on the road," she said.

"Ready, Ahnd?"

Ahnd turned the camera toward Trib, then counted down.

"Hi, friends!" Trib yelled as he walked to the edge of the presenter's booth with the DJ's equipment set up.

The crowd burst into cheers. One teen jumped up and yelled, "Can't stop the Trib." He was infectious and soon the crowd was jumping and chanting for Trib.

They were right. Not tonight. Tonight, nothing could

stop Trib. He was Tribinius Cantus, master of Ementhium. Trib hopped up on the DJ's table, and Ahnd adjusted, then Trib tapped his wrist pad to trigger his Inves' helmet—hiding the source of his power tonight—and slipped on his AIR glasses. Extending his arms, he said, "Ementhe Enterprises gives us the weather we need to be comfortable, clean, and happy. Tonight, we let it snow stars. Tonight, we rock this track!"

He thrust some pure Ementhium vapor out of his body and through his AIR glasses. The glasses were turned off and ignored the burst of vapor, letting it flow through into the night air. The light bent, creating thousands of little twinkling golden stars that tumbled to the ground. The stars bounced off the ground, high into the air, then rapidly grew bright as they burned out.

People stuck their hands out and let the stars bounce off of their skin. Some oohed while others ahhed, laughing with amusement at the magical stars.

That wasn't going to be his only trick of the night. Trib pumped a little more vapor through his device and cast a hologram around him that put him in a magician's outfit, complete with a custom-crafted suit, tie, bright red silk handkerchief coming out of his front pocket, and top hat.

"Have we got a show for you tonight," he said, grabbing his top hat and swirling it down around in front of him as he took a bow. "DJ VaporLight, please get this party started!"

The beats hit hard as DJ VaporLight screamed into the microphone. "Can't stop the Trib!"

The crowd roared as the stars changed color in time with the music, waves of light streaking through the twinkling rain. People danced, shaking their arms in the air and spinning about, then Trib grabbed the handkerchief from his pocket, spun it around, and shoved it into his hat. He kept his arm in his hat, spinning it around as if trying to find something, secretly releasing a stream of vapor, then smiled and pulled his hand out. Huge swaths of silks exploded out of the hat and spread out, flying towards the revelers. The silks firmed underneath them and lifted them up, bringing dancers into the air. They screamed with delight.

With a flourish, he produced a deck of cards masterfully spread out. He admitted to relying on the hologram machine for that. He might have unlimited power, but he didn't know how to fully use it. Swaying his hand back and forth, he forced Ementhium into the cards so that they grew bigger with each swing of his hand, then launched the cards up into the air. He pulled on the vapor connecting them to him, and they landed on edge, standing tall, then started dancing to the music. Some dancers grabbed the cards by the upper corners and started dancing with them. Somehow he felt connected to it all, in control of it all; Ementhium was his.

Trib tossed his top hat out into the sky with a shot of Ementhium. It grew to be the height of an adult and the width of twenty guys, then landed and spun into place, top up. Trib jumped up onto the rim, then hopped into the hat, bouncing up out of it and landing back on the rim.

"Trampoline, anyone?"

Dozens of people stormed the rim and jumped in, bouncing out and screaming with delight. Trib laughed, then twisted around and started dancing. Through the crowd, he caught Liv. He'd forgotten about her for a moment while he was a master of everything around him. How could he have forgotten Liv? She waved at him, obviously perturbed and seriously trying to fake being totally at ease.

Trib hopped down, then suddenly felt dizzy. He tried to steady himself, but it hit him that he had lost control of his body. He couldn't even command his legs. Trib collapsed into Coach Xius' arms.

"Whoa there, son," Coach said, hefting Trib's largely metallic body up. "Congratulations. You're in," he said with a laugh.

"In a daze," Trib said.

"It'll fade. Just stop using your vapor."

"The party," Trib said, then laid his head down and passed out.

RECOVERY

Trib blinked. His appendages were hanging off of him like the dead weights they were, pulling on his limbs, and his body was sore. He moaned and flexed his body, pulling himself back together again and vaguely registering the soft cushions of a couch under his body.

"He's awake," Coach Xius said.

Ahnd and Liv appeared, hovering over Trib.

"You okay?" Liv said.

Okay? Why wouldn't he be okay? He just felt a little hazy. The world still didn't make sense. And where was he? He shifted his body back and forth and recognized the couch. Was he in Coach's office?

"He'll be fine. Just give him a few minutes, kids."

"Are you going to tell us what happened now?"

Liv was being demanding and a little rude. That wasn't like her. Wait. It was coming back to him. The party. The power. The Ementhium. He had used too much too fast. He could feel that now and understood it.

"I burned it too fast, right?"

"I see you're coming back to us. Yes. The vapor on the market is thin enough that you can use it as fast as you want, but you were glowing, so your father showed you the Source."

"I'm not supposed to talk about it."

"No need to worry. I've studied this for a long time. I already know the corporations' secrets."

"How did you know?"

"That you were having a party? I told you your audience isn't all sixteen-year-olds."

"That I would collapse."

"Everyone does. It's a rite of passage, a hazing, you might say."

"He knew?"

"Your father? He did it, too. Everyone does. So, yes, he knew, but that doesn't make it bad."

"What else do you know about Ementhium?" Trib asked, pushing against the couch and forcing his muscles to sit up.

"It is not the most powerful vapor. It is powerful in many areas, but every vapor has its own power."

"Which is the most powerful?"

"Over 1100 years ago, Alexander Reyes had all nine vapors. It is said that with them, he was able to form a tenth. The tenth made him a god on Earth. With that vapor, he brought the people of Earth together to form a constitutional corporatocracy. The united people won out, though, forming our current government, rule by the corporations with the permission of the people. And when they overthrew him, Alexander Reyes's power couldn't protect him from the guile of the people. He was deposed and his property split between his nine daughters."

"I knew most of that, but not about the tenth vapor. Where'd you hear that?"

"You wouldn't believe me if I told you, but that's why no one person controls two corporations. It prevents another Alexander Reyes from rising. The law is misplaced. Alexander Reyes could harness all nine vapors naturally. You need that *and* all the vapors to make the tenth vapor."

"I'm happy with the three I can control, and this Ementhium is like a drug. I can't get enough of it."

"How much did you burn?"

"About a third," Trib said, rubbing his eyes.

"Don't fill up. If you do, it'll mix with the vapor in you and weaken it. Just don't release it too fast or you'll be out again."

"What else should I know?"

"For now, know that you've started down a path which leads to deeper and darker secrets. It is going to challenge who you are. Just remember that everything exists for a reason.”

“Who was your favorite teacher, Coach? You’re mine. I really appreciate you.”

“Everyone has taught me something, but I wasn’t always receptive to learning.”

“Five mill,” Ahnd said.

“Viewers? That’s awesome.”

“It is except for one. Your father. He sent for you as soon as you woke up. He sounded mad,” Liv said.

“He always sounds mad or disappointed,” Trib said. “I guess I should go see him. Thanks, Coach.”

“Anytime, son. I’m always here for my kids.”

Trib’s father was smiling when Trib entered his office. It didn’t look good on him.

“You didn’t do bad. I was worse,” Caran said.

“What’d you do?”

“I proposed to your mother.”

“With the power?”

“The power of a god used to seduce a woman. Can you think of a better way to do it?”

Trib chuckled, a little embarrassed to hear his father talking about his mother like that.

“I passed out.”

“We all do. She thought I was drunk and turned me

down."

"How old were you?"

"Seventeen. Once I explained it to her, she thought it was cute and accepted my proposal."

"So, what's next?"

"You like to party. You're going to the party in a couple of weeks. Bring your friends, but get them up to snuff. I will have my house putting on a good show."

Trib nodded.

"And you're going to start attending board meetings. You need to learn the people, not just the vapor."

Trib nodded.

"And, son, I'm proud of you. You could have done a lot of things with that power. You made a fair choice."

"Thanks."

"Thanks for what?" the male voice said.

Trib left, caught up in thought. Board meetings? Somehow that made his decision real, more so than the pure Ementhium. He'd never liked school and wasn't good at it. He'd only gone on to core from basic because his parents insisted and he didn't even finish that. Most people had a basic education. The top third were mostly those with core education, then the highly educated who lived in Alexandria. And now he was going to be in board meetings and have to learn how to operate a business. It was a little overwhelming.

Something caught him by the throat, killing his thoughts as much as his breath.

"There *she* is," said the giant with cauliflower ears.

Trib choked, but shook his head, a seriousness coming to him that made the behemoth think for a second. Trib threw his arms down and relaxed his body as he released pure Ementhium into the air. He was connected to it still, and he was its master.

Commanding the vapor, it rose into the air and a deep chill ran through that block of the temperature-controlled city. Above them, clouds formed in the cloudless city, and a lightning bolt shot between them. Ice rain poured down, surrounding his attacker while leaving the rest of the city untouched, then Trib caused the vapor to solidify the rain. The rain quickly froze from the ground up, droplets stacking on each other until a block of ice surrounded the man and left his extended arm exposed to air.

The man's grip relaxed on Trib's neck, and Trib stepped away. The ice was crystal clear and the look of mortification on the man's face equally so. Trib shook his head, then continued on his way home, leaving the man to freeze.

He could really do anything. What should he do with the remainder of this pure Ementhium? He wasn't sure, but he wanted it to be fantastic.

As he walked, the man's face filled his mind. What

would happen to him? He couldn't escape. The man would die. Maybe he was already dead. He probably was. Trib had killed a man. Yes, he could do anything. But that face. Would it ever go away? Trib had to tell himself that it was just ice. The man could break out. It would melt before he died. Yeah, that was it. Or was it? His mind raced back and forth between the two possibilities.

Kicking back in her recliner with her visor on to mask her nervousness, Liv thought while she waited for Trib. She didn't mind waiting for him. She knew what she was going to say, and it was going to change everything. For the better or the worse. She was sure it was going to be for the better. She'd thought about it.

Trib smiled at her the way he smiled at the camera. He'd given her presents. He hadn't found another girl. And he was always kind to her; he respected her as a trixer. All that had to mean something.

Of course, it could go for the worse. In the worst case, he would dump her as a friend. The likelihood of that happening was zilch. The real question was if it would hurt their relationship...their friendship. When it came down to it, Liv decided that Trib valued their friendship more than losing it.

Trib burst in the door

"Liv! Ahnd!" he shouted. "I just killed a guy."

Liv felt the wind get knocked out of her. So much for

what she had to say. It would have to wait.

"Really? How? What happened?" Liv said.

Ahnd looked up from his visisheet and gave Trib a considered look, then shook his head.

"Nah. Didn't. Wrong look," Ahnd said.

"Well, I left him to die. He's freezing to death in a block of ice."

"You have to get him out," Liv said.

"I can't. If I do, he'll kill me."

"Ice a guy, gonna run, not fight," Ahnd said. "Block of ice, bro?"

Trib shrugged. "First thing that came to mind."

"Gotta get him out."

"Yes, let's go," Trib said, tugging his jacket taut. "Now."

They ran down the street and stopped a block away from the Pad as a puddle surrounded the man in ice. Liv and Ahnd looked up at the sky, looked at Trib, then looked at each other.

Trib walked around the block of ice, then reached out and touched it, pouring energy from his body into his arm and out of his fingertips. The vapor crawled along the surface of the ice in a line, then striated like a lightning bolt into the block of ice, sheering it in half. The cauliflower ear guy collapsed to his knees, wrapping his hands around his shaking body.

"Trib. Help him."

"What can I do?"

"Warm him up," she said, slapping his shoulder.

Trib eased out vapor, and the man closed his eyes, basking in the warmth. The cloud of vapor vanished as the man stopped shivering. He opened his eyes and stared at Trib with utter fear. He was a man who feared nothing. Except, now, Trib. Liv felt for him and went over and gave him a hug.

"What's your name?" she asked.

"Avery."

"I'm Livia, Avery. You're going to be okay."

Wary, he said, "Thanks." He looked over at Trib and whispered to Liv, "What is he?"

"Tribinius. That's the best way to describe him. You two should talk. Tribinius! Come here."

Trib walked over, giving Avery a grim look, but smiling when he turned his attention to Liv. "Yeah?"

"Meet Avery. Avery, meet Tribinius. All his friends call him Trib."

"He's not my friend," Trib said.

"You attacked me."

"After you hit a girl."

"I lost my cool. It happens. Don't need some kid jumping in to prove me wrong."

"Maybe, but—"

"No 'buts'. Truce?" Avery said, swinging his hand out to shake on it.

Trib paused for a moment, then grabbed Avery's hand and gave it a firm shake.

"Truce."

As they shook hands, Avery looked at Trib like he was some sort of ghoul capable of mysterious magic.

"Good. You're friends," Liv said with plenty of joyful exuberance. Her Inves buzzed at her and Liv checked it. "I have to go. I have an appointment with your mom, Trib."

She was excited about this meeting. It was her first meeting to learn about fashion. She hoped that Mrs. Cantus wouldn't be condescending, and she hoped to learn enough to impress Trib. She had to show him she was worthy of him.

CHARACTER CUT

Liv had never seen Trib's mansion before. It was an actual house with more rooms than she could count, and it was surrounded by trees and landscaping. The house itself was white with an ornate façade. There was something about it that communicated to her, but she didn't know what it was saying.

The door opened and Evie Lynn Cantus stepped out, waving with one hand and a turn of her wrists as if she were royalty. Liv started for her, but Evie Lynn held up a hand signaling her to stay, then joined Liv.

"Good to see you, dear," Evie Lynn said.

"You too, dear," Liv said. She was so nervous. She was in so far over her head that she felt like swimming was drowning.

"You don't call me dear, dear. You can just refer to me as Mrs. Cantus, or Evie Lynn."

"Yes, Mrs. Cantus."

"I think we're going to be friends, so how about we stick with Evie Lynn?"

Liv blushed. "Yes, Evie Lynn. You have a miraculous house."

"Thank you. It's pre-aught. Do you see how sensuous the curves are? They almost suggest the flowing form of a woman, but without being explicit. An Istael Burkesy original. Bought in pieces from very selective sellers. Only corporation executives can own them. It's part of the contract.

"Liv, you're about to enter a very exclusive world. It is alluring, but it can be your undoing. Just remember, the cut is the character, and the character is the cut. You buy what you must, not what you want. How do you want to be perceived? Which level of society do you fit in? Everything you do reflects that choice."

"I'll never be able to do this. My family is poor, Mrs... Evie Lynn. This isn't me."

"You are who you choose to be, dear. Come. Let's go inside."

Inside was a streamlined, clean, jetliner-optimized home that flowed in curves. The counters were cut at angles which melded into the walls to form complementary angles with doors. Together, they looked like an undulating river. The walls were metal and curved along the wall. It was as if the whole house were designed in one sitting. It took her breath away.

"It is best to look appreciative, not overawed," Evie Lynn said. "We're just like any family, but we are part of the upper class, so we express it differently."

Liv tried to put on an appreciative face, but she was sure the awe still came through.

"Your appearance," Evie Lynn said as she led Liv toward a back room, "speaks volumes. If you're unkempt, people will know that you don't care for yourself. If you're last year, they will see you as uninvolved. If you're...well, you get the point. How you look and how you carry yourself define how people will treat you."

Liv nodded, but didn't agree. She judged people on who they were, not what they looked like. If she'd gone on appearance alone, she'd have never become friends with Ahnd. And Trib would have never become friends with her. Still, she was here to learn more about how to seduce Trib and fit into his lifestyle. Maybe he saw her through these colored lenses. Maybe that's why he hadn't approached her yet.

Evie Lynn stepped up to a large door which rotated open as she approached, exposing a large walk-in closet with hundreds of outfits, shoes, hats, and everything imaginable. Groups of hanging dresses, skirts, and blouses were sorted by color, each group undoubtedly representing a season from the various tones of each batch. It was a breathtaking display of order, taste, and perfection.

"Never be caught with your mouth open," Evie Lynn said, reaching out and pressing Liv's chin.

Liv closed her mouth and blushed. "I've never seen..."

"Remember what I said about displaying overawe."

"Yes. It's impressive. A nice selection," Liv answered, trying to put on airs.

Evie Lynn smiled and selected a flowing, lilac-colored dress with a tight bust that exposed a little shoulder, but not enough to be too distracting for males. "Dresses are inherently sexist. So is your body. Accentuate your womanhood; don't shy away from it. It is in your best interest to be the best woman you can be. Take this dress. What does it say to you?"

Liv took a deep breath, pursed her lips, ready to pronounce judgment and said, "Womanly, but distanced. It says I'm everything you want and I'm out of your reach."

"Excellent, but it says more. That's what you're going to learn. Brands have meaning. This is a Jordan River. Jordan River is an excellent brand, but not the most luxurious. Known for its fluid form, it suggests motion, activity, liveliness. The brand helps define the dress, and that helps define how others perceive you."

For the next three hours, Evie Lynn poured information into Liv, and Liv was a sponge. Maybe if she learned to live in Trib's world, he would be more willing to accept her. She could do this. It was just another way of thinking, and it wasn't the us-vs-them attitude of her own class.

"Since you're going to be assisting my son at the office. You'll need something appropriate to wear," she said in a conclusory tone, then fished three outfits from her closet. "They're older, but they'll convey the most important thing to those around you: my approval. I'll have to take you shopping, of course, but you must demonstrate progress first."

"Yes, Evie Lynn," Liv said, reaching out for the clothing. The dresses were too short for Evie Lynn, but they were the perfect height for Liv. They had similar body types, too, so the fit looked like it would be comfortable. Impressively, the cut told the character: competently in charge.

After trying on a few outfits, Liv opted for a break. She sat down on the bedroom bench next to Evie Lynn.

"I can see why he likes you," Evie Lynn said.

"Evie Lynn, I can't believe you would go there," Liv said, trying to sound like she was upper class.

"Girlfriends don't lie to girlfriends. It's a well-known secret that you two are in love, but haven't accepted it."

Liv blushed so hard she thought her skin fluoresced.

"Now, now, dear. There's nothing to be embarrassed about. Except maybe how long you're letting him wait."

"Wait, what?" Liv said, shocked and forgetting her manners.

Evie Lynn laughed. "Men think they are in charge because they run things, but they're never in charge when it comes to love. Go with your gut, dear. He won't leave you. He loves you as much as you do him."

"How do you know?"

"A mother knows her son. I can see it in how he looks at you."

Liv cheeks reddened again, but took a breath and calmed herself.

"You'll see. Convincing yourself to do it is always the hardest part. We convince ourselves to do a lot of things for the men in our lives."

She was more eloquent, but it sounded a lot like the advice her own mother would give her. Liv liked Evie Lynn. She scooted closer to her and put her arm around her soon-to-be boyfriend's mom.

"Thank you, Evie Lynn."

Evie Lynn took a deep breath and stood. "Shall we talk accouterments?" she said, turning to face Liv.

"If you tell me what that means," Liv said, not sure if she should understand the word.

"The things you wear other than clothes, dear. Jewelry, for example."

"Oh, yes. Accouterments," Liv replied as if the word

were obvious.

She took Liv over to a dresser and opened up a jewelry box of untold riches. It sparkled like Trib's eyes on a starry night. Evie Lynn looked at Liv's ears and nodded.

"You're pierced, so that's good. You're tall, so you can wear longer earrings but not too long, mind you. I recommend something of this length," she said, holding up a pair of breathtaking emerald cluster earrings. "You will also want a necklace," she said, turning back to her box. She lifted up a yellow diamond riviere necklace and held it up to Liv's neck. "Yes, that will do."

"Thank you, Evie Lynn," Liv said, taking the necklace and clasping it on.

Evie Lynn smiled, then held out her hand, opening it to reveal three rings. "These should fit and complete your outfit. These are for the office only, dear. It wouldn't do to have you running around the streets like this."

"Yes, Evie Lynn."

"It is time for lunch. Are you hungry?"

Liv nodded.

Chef Truvi prepared them an elaborate but sparse meal. A dozen little platters with different concoctions. Liv didn't know any of them, but Evie Lynn explained, including what choosing each meant to how others perceived her.

"I had him prepare this especially for you. These are hors d'ouevers you'll see at parties."

The one with some kind of ham and white cheese was her favorite, so she ate two. She only had two of the starchier ones. Any more, according to Evie Lynn, would signify that she wasn't watching her figure. The bacon wrapped shrimp with a sprig of something green was her second favorite. She had two of those, too.

Drinking, of course, also said something about you. There were five drinks presented for each of them.

"These are alcoholic drinks. Have you ever been drunk before?"

"No, but I have had a drink once."

"These won't be that pleasant. They're made of hard alcohol, but not much. You must never be drunk in public, and I don't recommend it in private. You know my son is bipolar, right?"

"Yes, of course."

"He can have an episode at any time. He needs someone more stable than he is to be there for when he can't be there for himself."

Again, she sounded like her mother, but more eloquent. Her mother would laugh and say, "Men need women care for them. Can't care themselves."

Liv nodded.

"Have you ever seen him have an episode? Oh, yes. I

remember now. I've seen you at the mental hospital. You came to see him."

"If you're asking if I understand Trib, no, I don't. I know him well enough to protect him, but I don't think anyone can understand Trib, even Trib."

"Good point."

"If you're asking if I love him, the answer is yes. I know he has his problems. I know he doesn't have arms and legs. I know he needs care, but I was raised to care for my husband." Liv caught herself on that last word and blushed hard, swallowed, then continued. "But I also know he's caring. It's pure honesty. When he focuses on you, it's like you're his whole world and he'll fight to keep you part of it. When he's taking his meds, he's exciting and great to be around. The secret to understanding Trib is to know he can't be understood. I don't know how to say it better."

"I would say you've done an excellent job," Evie Lynn said. "To have the approval of family when entering a relationship is key. If they do not accept you into the fold, then you're blackballed from any other fold. Livia Yasserton, you have my acceptance. Welcome to the fold."

"Oh, my gosh. I don't know what to say, Mrs...Evie Lynn."

"Thank you is enough."

"Thank you, but I haven't even asked him. Or he

hasn't asked me. Both...I'm stuttering."

"Yes, you are, but never point that out. Just overcome it," she said. "It *is* contingent on you two actually getting together. Take your time, dear."

She was right. Liv could take her time, but like Evie Lynn had also said, that time had come. Next time she was alone with him, a crazy story about killing a man wouldn't be enough to stop her.

AIR OF THE HEIR

With Liv on his right and Ahnd to his left, Trib strutted down Ementhe Enterprises only slightly behind his dad. Trib had dressed in an impressive cut built for his Inves and Ahnd was Ahnd, but Livia wore a lively light blue dress with curves that commanded obedience and jewelry that made her shine. She was distracting, at the least.

"Most decisions are routine. They come to you to evade responsibility, not to be given answers," Caran preached.

"What about the non-routine questions?" Trib asked.

"Your subordinates come to you to be given answers *and* pass the responsibility to you. Every decision you ever make will have positive and negative consequences. Look at them and decide what you're willing to accept, then invest yourself in the answer."

Caran continued on quietly, pacing more than going

anywhere, until his secretary buzzed him.

"Mr. Efferson is here to see you, sir."

"I'll meet him in my office," he answered, then led them to the CEO's office.

A short, frumpy old man hefted himself through the door. His triple chin jiggled as he spoke.

"Mr. Cantus," he said, "there's been a misprint on the order of ten million units."

Caran lifted his chin and addressed Trib. "You can handle this one."

Trib blinked. "What the? Okay. Um, what kind of misprint."

"Their solid teal branded color experienced a printing error. They came out rainbow colored."

"Aren't you empowered to handle this?"

"Not when the cost is millions of coin. Normally, we'd just destroy the lot. I need your permission to destroy a lot this size."

"Don't destroy it. Increase the price and sell it as a limited edition. People will love it."

Mr. Riverside looked at Caran, but Caran stared blankly until Mr. Riverside nodded and stepped out.

"Well done. You just saved the company 100 million coin."

"Two hundred plus. The amount I saved, plus the amount I earned."

Caran grinned. "Very good. Never let someone undervalue your contributions." He addressed Ahnd and Liv, also turning his attention to the guards at the door, "I will speak with Tribinius alone."

Liv and Ahnd looked to Trib, and Trib nodded. "I'll catch up to you at the Pad."

Liv and Ahnd left along with the two guards standing at the door.

"Tribinius," Caran said as the door shut. "I am glad to see you are taking your inheritance seriously. Much rides on your success."

"You could have said that in front of Liv and Ahnd. Why private?"

"You're too young, I'm sure, but it is what it is." Caran sighed, then continued. "There is a council of the corporations. We cooperate and work toward a common goal."

"What's that got to do with me?"

"Your recent actions have been noticed. You've posed a threat to the balance we have established. Son, I need you to focus on what matters: your future, that girl, your inheritance."

"Is this a threat? And what do you mean about that girl?"

"Instability is a threat. I'm only asking you to keep doing what you are doing—taking Ementhe Enterprises and your role seriously," he answered, ignoring Trib about Liv.

"Dad, I'm going to keep being me."

"Be careful, Tribinius. There are forces here much greater than you understand."

"Yeah. I've been told. Are we done?"

"Yes. For now."

LOVELY LIVIA

"I'm here for my next lesson," Liv said, standing at the door of the Cantus home.

"Yes, of course, dear. Come in. I trust you're doing well?"

"I am. Thank you for asking, Evie Lynn. The dance is tomorrow."

"Yes, it is. That brings us to today's lesson," Evie Lynn said, stopping at her large walk-in closet and letting the doors open.

The closet was less intimidating, but still awe-inspiring for Liv. She had a better understanding of what was in the closet, but it felt like it would take years to understand every cut and brand. Evie Lynn stepped into the closet and spun a couple of racks of clothes around, pulling one rack from out behind the others.

"Try this on. We'll see how that goes," she said, selecting a sequined gown that was too short for Evie

Lynn but looked the right height for Liv. "I wore that in high school."

"You save your clothes?" Liv said, slipping into the sheer clothing.

"Some. If they have meaning."

"What's this one mean?" Liv bounced up and down, tugging at the gown and straightening herself into it. "It fits great."

Evie Lynn blushed, covering her mouth as reserved surprise painted her face a rose color.

"Yes, well. Let's find one which can have some meaning for you."

She ruffled through the rack of her teen clothes, selecting a few dresses, reminiscing over a couple, then turning and held out one final dress.

"And here's the one for the ball, dear. This has special meaning for me. Now, it will have special meaning for you, since this is your first ball."

The dress was fantastic, and Liv fell instantly in love, but Evie Lynn didn't give her a chance to relish it.

"You will need jewelry and shoes. Unfortunately, we don't have time to do a proper job of your makeup. I really need to take you on a shopping trip. Fortunately, you're a beautiful young woman, so you'll do fine, but let's do some touchups."

Liv followed Evie Lynn to her vanity, where she

daubed a little powder on Liv's face, refining her youthful blemishes.

Evie Lynn stood back, head high, and smiled. "Yes, perfect. I knew you wouldn't take much, but just wait until we get you a professional job. My son won't be able to contain himself."

Liv blushed and bowed her head. "Really, Evie Lynn."

"You know where the shoes are. Make yourself at home."

Liv's heart dropped with excitement. There were at least eight dozen pairs of shoes arranged on racks. She matched them against the dress and found a perfect complement to the dress.

"Excellent. You have a natural sense of style. Those are the shoes I wore with that dress."

Liv grinned with pride, slipping into the shoes, then struck a pose for Evie Lynn. "What do you think?"

"I think my son is a fool. He should have asked you out already," she said, shocking Liv. Without missing a heartbeat, she continued, "I set some jewelry out for you on the nightstand."

DREAM STREAM

Trib stared in the mirror, refining his smile. He wanted everything to be perfect. But why did he think he needed to work on his smile? He had that down pat. It was jitters. He was nervous. He smiled mockingly at himself, perked his little heart up and gave himself a wink. He had this.

Trib straightened his tie and lifted his chin high. This was the perfect cut for the occasion. It said reserved, suave. He was cool, calm, collected, and confident all in one. He wasn't fond of pure white. It conflicted with his complexion, so he'd ordered off white and accentuated it with a light green bowtie. It said young and energetic. It was everything Trib wanted to say.

Well, with his clothes. He'd thought about it, and twirling his fingers around the small box of promise rings in his pocket, he thought about it again. Livia could put up with him. He was sure of that, or maybe not sure, but pretty sure. He did have some seriously bad times. But did she want to? Would she say yes? What if she didn't? What would it do to their friendship? He might not get a second chance.

He rehearsed the words over and over, making himself confident and committing the words to memory. He knew exactly what he wanted to say and had thought about every word more than once. It had the meaning he wanted it to have, and would swoon any girl. This couldn't go wrong. No, he was Tribinius Cantus. This would go perfectly.

Trib flipped his wrist up and pulled up Ahnd on a call.

"I'm going to ask her out at the party tonight. I want you to stream it."

"Private thing, bro."

"Me? Private?" Trib laughed. "Do I know you?"

Ahnd shrugged. "Your girl. Got your back."

Tribinius closed the holocall and opened up a new call to his father.

"Tribinius? Is everything alright?"

"Yeah. I'm going to ask her tonight. I need permission to broadcast it. Can you hook me up?"

Caran pulled his head back as if considering, then leaned forward with a grin that didn't suit his face. "You've kept your word so far. I will arrange it. Make it special, son."

"Thanks, Dad," Trib said and dropped the connection.

Peeking through the driver's seat, he saw familiar buildings passing. The time was here. The car pulled into the driveway. He hadn't chosen just any Mæssan car. This year's Model M, the signature series. Someone opened his door for him and he stepped out to applause, Ahnd getting out of the seat behind him and coming up with the camera.

Trib's Inves beeped. He looked at it and grinned. It was a message from his dad. His dad had come through.

"Hi, friends. I'm here on the red carpet to tonight's gala. I promise you there will be a treat for tuning in tonight."

"No cameras," a guard said, reaching for Ahnd's camera.

Ahnd deftly angled back and dodged the guard's grip while keeping the camera on Trib.

Trib winked in the camera and held up his Inves. "Check the credentials," he said as he held up permission from the CEO of Ementhe Enterprises to record tonight's event.

They scanned the code, waited for verification, then waved them on.

"Can't stop the Trib," Trib said into the camera. "We came prepared for tonight."

Trib looked around for Liv, but in the sea of known

faces, she was not among them, though Anton was. Anton was for later in the show. He needed to find Liv, but his show had to go on, so Trib gave a bow to the camera and twirled onto the dance floor, coming up on a group of older women dancing together. He joined in and they rooted him on, swinging their hips to match his dancing. Shifting to another party, a couple, he danced alongside them, nodding his head in a bow to the woman, then the man. He swirled the woman around, then grabbed the man's hands and danced. They laughed as Trib spun around and ended up solo....

Not solo. Alone with her. Alone with Liv. She stood there in an all white dress that draped down just below her ankles, golden embroidery and diamonds peppering the dress's lining. Her makeup and jewelry made her look years older and much hotter. Trib knew this dress as well as he knew Liv, and she made it magical.

The dress gave Trib courage. He doubted his mother had told her what the dress meant, but it was a message of encouragement to Trib.

"Tribinius," Liv started, but Trib held a finger up to her mouth.

"Livia Yasserton. I...I..." Oh, no. He was drawing a blank. What was it he had decided to say? What were those words again? He couldn't remember and he was choking. He was ruining this. "I love you. Will you be my girlfriend?"

Well, that didn't come out right. It was what it was, though. He'd said it. Ahnd was now circling around with the camera, pointing it straight at Liv, who completely ignored it.

"Yes," she said. "It's about time you asked."

A level of relief and relaxation came over him that could move a city off its foundation. She had wanted him to ask. She had said yes. This was the best night of his life. He leaned forward and picked her up, spinning her around, then lowered her so face to his, then pressed lips together. It was sloppy and a little awkward, but it worked. He finally had the girl.

"Oh..." Trib said, setting her down and taking a step away. He concentrated some of the pure Ementhium still in his system and sucked at the light in the room, drawing its radiance toward the pair of them. It drew everyone's attention, and in the center of the bright shine, his hand came up with the pair of promise rings.

"Livia Yasserton, I promise to be yours now and forever," he said.

Tears filled her eyes and she reached out, grabbed a promise ring and slipped it on her finger. He put on the other one, then let the light fade back to its place.

"She said yes!" he said.

Everyone clapped as if she'd just said yes to marriage. He reached out and offered his hand, then spun her into him and back out as they broke into dancing.

They danced and danced, drawing closer to each other, her scent more intoxicating than ever. They danced until she begged for a chance to get something to drink. He kissed her, they both blushed, and she went to get something to drink.

"Out now. Trib's girl. Ton of hate mail." Ahnd chuckled, shaking his head. "Congrats, bro."

"Views?"

"Five million. Consistent."

"Gentlemen," Anton said.

"Anton, my man. I've been waiting for you to say hi."

"Why in the world for?"

"People hated playing games with me in core. They knew I'd always win. I didn't always win, but I won enough of the time that people thought I did. Tonight, I win big. Why play games with me?"

"I knew he knew," the male voice said, except it wasn't any male voice. Trib recognized the voice now.

Then you know what you're in for, Trib thought at the voice.

"I do," Anton said, then things became awkward. He had answered their thought conversation. "Don't do it. I'll give you what you really want."

"What's that?"

He nodded at Ahnd, the camera specifically. Trib signaled to Ahnd and he turned the camera around, focusing on the party.

"I can show you the real source of Ementhium, but it's risky. Like, your-dad-might-disown-you risk."

"And why do I want this?"

"It's the source of *pure Ementhium*. You didn't like your first taste?"

"I've seen the source. Touched it."

"You never touched it. You didn't see the Source. You saw the prison. I can't talk more about it here. Your pad in two days, okay?"

"Okay, but you'd better not be playing with me."

"Not me. Everyone else."

And with that, he slipped back into the crowd and disappeared just as Liv returned with drinks in hand. Ahnd brought the camera back around while Trib wrapped arms with Liv and they tried to give each other a sip of a golden liquid. Trib smiled when he saw the drink and almost spilled his all over her.

The night dimmed down and Trib said goodbye to his stream viewers. Ahnd vanished shortly thereafter, saying something about a date, leaving Trib and Liv alone.

Trib looked at Liv, his girlfriend, with new eyes. Eyes beholden with a love he'd suppressed far too long. He wanted her in every way. Wanted to hold her, touch her, care for her.

"Let's stay at the Pad tonight."

She grinned and nodded.

CONFESSIONS

Two days later, Anton showed up at the Pad dressed to the nines. His outfit said *better than you, got somewhere more exclusive to be, but I've lowered myself for the occasion.* Trib smiled as Liv let Anton in, then took her place in her recliner, which she'd pushed up next to Trib's. They curled fingers together as they sat, and with his free hand, Trib waved at a misty wall in front of him.

"Just so I know you get me," Trib said, and Liv broadcast the still captured just after Anton took his hood off.

"I know what you have on me. I know where I made my mistake. Going to offer me a seat?"

Trib grabbed a chair from the dining room and set it in front of the recliners. "Please, do."

"Record this, please, Mr. Mesixia," Anton said. "I want to make sure you know I know how well screwed I am."

Ahnd popped up the camera and signaled to Trib that he was recording, not broadcasting.

"I, Anton Variega, stole the Ementhian and made it look like Tarah Livings had done it. The full story is that I stole it not knowing it was against the law. I mean, to own two corporate medallions. I knew stealing was against the law, but I thought if I had two of them, no one could stop me and I would inherit two corporations. I was wrong and tried to cover it up by setting up Tarah Livings."

He took a deep breath, then said, "You can stop recording now."

Ahnd set the camera down and Anton continued.

"I'm sorry that I stole your medallion and setup someone else. I've come to take responsibility for my actions."

"Nope. Evading. Want help," Ahnd said.

"Yes," Anton responded plainly.

"When you saw the source of Ementhium, you did not touch it. Your father told you not to touch it, right?"

"Right," Trib said.

"It's always a matter of time before you do touch it. They just like to be ready when you do. I touched it. I tripped and fell into it.

"When I did, something inside of it reached out to me. A man who was a lion below the torso, flexing his muscles hard as he held up the city. He oozed Mæssium. It radiated off his skin and out to the orb containing him. What was odd was that he was in a large room, but the Source is so small. Our Source isn't a source; it's a prison. I'll bet yours is too."

"What's your point?"

"Wait until your father gives you the speech."

"Why can I hear your voice in my head?"

Anton's eyes sparkled with enlightenment. "You can hear me? I can hear you. I thought it was you doing it. Punishing me."

"Can you hear a girl?"

"Sometimes, yeah. That's not you?"

"No. I thought it was you. Maybe it's her."

Anton looked at Liv and Ahnd, both looking a little awkwardly at the exchange. "They didn't know?"

"They do now. Liv, Ahnd. We hear voices. I hear him, and he hears me. And we hear some girl, too."

"You hear girls in your head?" Liv said.

"No, just one."

"Who is she?"

"I don't know. You, Anton?"

"I'm afraid I don't. She seems familiar, but I can't place her. Maybe someone from a party?"

"I get that feeling, too."

"When do you hear her voice?" Liv said.

"I don't pick," Trib said. "Why?"

"Just wondering, is all."

"Oh. I get it. No. It's not like that. Right, Anton?"

"No. Random thoughts, not like typical boys thinking of girls," he said, snickering. "But now that I know she's as real as us. I'll be on the lookout."

"Got pure vape?" Ahnd asked.

"I'm getting low. I can only do one more trick, then I'll have to rely on my suit. What's the Ementhian have to do with it?"

"My guess is the same thing the Mæssium does with our source of vapor. It unlocks the jail," Anton said.

"Getting pure vapor is easy enough. We can fill up on pure vapor when we're near the Source. But I have to see this for myself, touch it myself," Trib said.

"How are you going to get in there?" Anton asked.

Trib smiled. "Do you know my catch phrase?"

"Can't stop the Trib?"

"Meet team Trib. The unstoppable team Trib."

Trib paced the Pad like he was crazy. His mind ran as fast as his feet shuffled. He wasn't acting cool. He was stressed, and that was coming out. He needed a plan, but first, he needed to decide if he was even going to do this.

It was like a dense fog blurred his vision—he couldn't think straight, couldn't really see straight, if he thought about it. Why was this so hard? He closed his eyes and squinched them tight, willing away the unclarity.

There it was in his memories. The words were coming back to him. "It's a prison." "...Unlocks the jail." These were actual spoken words, not overheard thoughts. Ementhe Enterprises had someone unjustly locked up.

That was all it took. The veil lifted. Trib knew the right thing to do.

"We're going in," he said.

"Yeah," Ahnd said, grunting.

"We know, Trib. We were just waiting for you to figure it out. We're already preparing."

Trib looked around and laughed. His friends knew him better than he knew himself.

"We're going to have to rely on some luck. I don't have a plan."

Ahnd grunted.

"It'll be okay, Trib. You'll come up with something. You always do. When do we go?"

"Tomorrow night."

Ahnd grabbed a few choice things from his backpack, the one he'd taken to Tacenteon. He hadn't returned it to the secured hole in his bedroom yet since Trib needed more and more protection lately. He slipped two blades and a couple of Grop bombs into his pockets. Nothing had gotten more serious than that, but today they were diving into someone's prison. Prisons were always guarded and dangerous. Ahnd grabbed the gun, then thought better of it and grabbed a hunting knife. It wasn't that anyone really hunted anymore, but the design was made to kill. Guns had a way of killing that knives didn't. Ways that Ahnd appreciated all too well.

"Ready?" Trib asked.

"Yeah. Sure, bro? Thinking better not ask questions."

"It's like Anton said. Sooner or later, we all do it. Why not sooner?"

Liv snuggled up next to Trib and kissed him. "I'm ready."

Trib blushed so delicately that if there were any girls around, they'd start fawning over him.

"Need a room?" Ahnd asked.

Trib laughed and Liv scowled. "Okay. Then, let's do this. Got the Brumenium?"

"I'll put it in my suit. I have space," Liv said, then grabbed the container of Brumenium and hooked it to her suit. The suit ate up the vapor, its fuel display changing to add the brown element. She waved her hand over the three of them, releasing the vapor and making it twinkle, then suddenly they couldn't see each other.

"Let's hold hands so we know where everyone is," Trib said.

Liv tapped Ahnd's hand. He assumed Trib had hers

and followed as she pulled, leading him out of the Pad and down the street. They crossed past the Lucky Lady and D&N's, then crossed the parking lot to the back entry to the shipping room. Liv entered the code, opening the door. They'd thought of using Trib's palm, but that might trigger an alert that he was where he wasn't supposed to be.

Ahnd surveyed the location. Still three unblocked exits and one stairway leading in both directions. He was fairly certain that the place was in exactly the same condition as the last time he was here, plus a little more dust.

Liv pulled him along into the elevator, inching their way along.

"There's no button," Trib whispered.

"To where?" Liv asked.

"The E floor. That's where we need to go."

"Does the override work for it?"

"No override either."

"Well, pfft."

"We can't go down. Need to find another way."

"Stairway on left," Ahnd said.

Holding hands, Ahnd led them to the stairway. They went down one floor, but there was no elevator there.

"Follow me," Trib said and pulled the trio train toward a far wall.

"This is where the elevator shaft is. This one will go all the way to the bottom. Hold on. I'm going to use the AIR."

The AIR module was seriously wicked tech, and not being able to see it used made its effect even more like magic. A hole suddenly appeared in the wall, opening to the bottom of the elevator shaft.

"Four stories," Trib said, then a stream of Ementhium vapor appeared, pouring down to the ground. Another burst of brighter Ementhium shot into the vapor and the mist solidified into a twisting rope with knots periodically positioned down the line.

"We'll rappel down. I'll call when I'm down."

"Me first," Ahnd said.

"Okay."

Ahnd walked carefully to the door, unable to see his friends and not wanting to knock one down the shaft, then took the rope and hopped out onto it, wrapping his feet around a knot. He relaxed his grip and slipped down to the next knot, then continued working his way down the rope, quickly sliding to the bottom.

"Down," he yelled up, then stepped back.

This misty teal room had no other exits and a glowing blue sphere in front of him. Ementhium flowed out of it like a wheezing breath, inconsistent and in bursts. The rest of the room was empty, sans some steel pillars holding the building up. Above the sphere, Ementhium rushed into a glass tube that went up story after story through the entire building. It was pretty cool, if somewhat barren.

A brown mist appeared over them and settled. The Brumenium did its magic, and they were all visible again.

"This is amazing, Trib! This is where all the Ementhium comes from?" Liv said in wonderment.

"Yes," Trib said with a serious look. He reached out, then shook his head. He detached an arm and handed it to Ahnd, then moved toward the sphere with the stump of his arm out. "I can tell I have to touch it with flesh. I don't know how."

Trib's nub touched the sphere and the whole room went bright. But not bright enough to blind Ahnd. Three people entered from the elevator, two who looked like guards and the other was Trib's dad.

Ahnd grabbed a Grop bomb and tossed it at their feet. They hadn't seen one before. They just looked at it and shrugged it off, then the drug began to take effect and they fell to the ground.

Caran Cantus didn't fall. He swept out with his arm in an overarching swoop and released bright Ementhium into the air. The Grop toxin stuck in place, then fell like little pebbles to the ground. He marched forward, and Ahnd ran in front of him while Liv was frozen in place, horror struck across her face like a slap caught in place.

As Ahnd slipped in front of Caran, the old man reached out and touched Ahnd, and a weave of metal wrapped around him, fixing him into the ground.

"Not tonight, son," Caran said, continuing to flow freely forward.

Caran placed both hands on Trib and jerked him free.

Trib came back gasping. He quickly caught his breath, then glared at his father with a full body fury that could pierce souls.

"Vapor comes from people. Slaves?"

"No. We all discover this at some point. It is our secret. You've shown these two too much."

"They can be trusted. They saved my life. Don't even begin to tell me who I can and cannot trust when you've been raising me to be a slave owner!"

"Fine. Bring them," he said, casting a little pure Ementhium at Ahnd.

The metal encasing around Ahnd became brittle, and Ahnd flexed, easily breaking it. Glaring at Caran, he joined them as they entered the elevator. Caran left the two guards to suffer the drug, and they ascended to the only other stop for this elevator: the top floor.

"You confessed back there, didn't you? You *are* a slaver."

Caran didn't respond. He sealed the door and closed the shades.

ANCIENT HISTORY

Caran took his seat behind his desk and motioned at the rest of the furniture for everyone else to sit.

"You will want to sit for this. In over 1100 years, only corporation heirs have heard what you are about to hear. Not even your mother knows this, Tribinius."

They sat down on the couch, Ahnd plopping and Liv taking a demure seat while Trib thumped down with an accusatory glare.

"Don't bullshit me, Dad. I've seen him."

And he had. When his arm touched the Ementhium sphere, Trib's mind was teleported inside, and he saw a naked blue man inside of a crystalline cave. The man's arms were raised and Ementhium flowed out of his hands and into the crystals.

"What are you doing?" Trib had asked the blue man.

"Saving the planet."

"How?"

"Preventing it from collapsing on me. If it collapses, I die; if I die, it dies."

"That's a lie. You're in a jail cell. I'm going to get you out."

"You can't. Or we all die. I have to save the planet."

The vision ended when his father pulled him back.

"Alexander Reyes discovered the nine vapors. That is true, but they weren't vapors. They were creatures from another planet or realm or somewhere. We don't really know. These creatures took on human-like forms. They claimed to be our creator, that they had been here from the beginning of Earth. When they learned Alexander Reyes could command all nine vapors, they tried to trap him with an elaborate plan, but he saw through their plan and built a city on top of each, casting a spell with the tenth vapor to seal them in forever. The Corporation was built from these nine cities until the people themselves turned on Alexander and broke his company up, one to each of his nine daughters. It is from them that we inherit our corporation. It is said that during each birth, he infused his daughters with a pure vapor, each getting a different one. Through their blood lineage comes our power to control Ementhium with the Ementhian, and it is how the other corporations work too."

"So, you are a slaver. But you're the slave master for a species from another planet!"

"We are part of that slavery. Without them, our city

falls. Without them, our people fall. We'd be sent back to the pre-aught era, before the vapor we thrive on. We need them as much as they need us."

"That doesn't make any sense. You're saying that because it might be an inconvenience to us, they must be slaves. Slavery is wrong for any reason."

"Would you give it all up? Give up your Inves suits? Your AIR module? Your hoverboards? AI-enabled cameras? Would you destroy everything that everyone else has over some notion of slavery? Besides, we didn't build their jail. What makes you think we can break them out of it?"

"Is this how you felt when we were kidnapped? When kids were killed? When I lost my siblings? You didn't put me in that jail, so how could you get me out?"

"Tribinius, that's not fair, and you know it. We paid to get you out."

"So, it was right to do something when it was your own son, but not when it's something like an alien?"

"Take some time to think about it. I think you'll find that we don't have a choice."

"I'll think about it," Trib said. And he would. For all of about one second. Yep. There it was. Decision made. His father was wrong and wouldn't accept that fact. It was time to exit stage left.

Trib stood, Liv and Alnd following suit.

"Sorry about the hole in your wall."

"Next time you want to go down there, just ask."

"Yes, father."

They left, and that's when the questions started coming. Mostly from Liv. Was he really going to think about it? What was he going to do? Aliens? Slave aliens?

"Trib!" Liv said, jumping in front of him. "Are you going to answer?"

"Yes. Yes, we're going to do something about it. Yes, the aliens might be upset when we free them, but, yes, the risk of doing the right thing is worth it."

"Rights crusade?" Ahnd said. "Glowing again."

"If you could have felt his pain, you... I don't have the right words. You would have to save him, too. It's just *that* wrong. And I know I'm glowing. When I touched the source, it powered me up."

They grew quiet until they got to the Pad door. It was late, but Trib needed to do something. "Liv. Can you get me Coach Xius' address?"

"Yeah," she said, instantly understanding.

The pitch of the roof cut a long slope across the sky, forming a modern skyline. Vibrant walls draped over fine edges like rich white linen sheets. It was smooth and exacting. Whiter than most houses, it stood out as a shiny diamond in the rough. Coach Xius had money to have a house like this. That, or he built it. Either way, it was impressive.

Coach opened the door, dressed in white and looking like someone from a martial arts movie. He smiled as warmly as ever.

"Trib. I see you found my home. Welcome. Come in."

Trib thought he had surprised Coach, but if there was any surprise, Coach didn't show it.

"No shoes."

"They're attached to my suit, Coach."

"Well, keep them on. This isn't a locker room."

If the outside didn't make it clear, the inside did: Coach liked white. From the carpet to the plush couches, it was all an inviting warm white.

"Please make yourself at home. How can I help you, son? You're glowing, so you've been near the Source," Coach said, taking a seat on a plush ivory couch.

"I want to tell you a story, Coach," Trib said, taking a seat on a couch across from Coach Xius.

Trib repeated the unbelievable story from his dad. He was pretty sure he got the details right, but Coach didn't seem shocked by it; he took it in stride.

"Did you get the sense that he was lying?" Coach said.

"No, but you can't read my dad."

"Well, intentionally or not, he wasn't telling the truth. It *is* the creator. We know exactly who it is."

Trib was pretty sure he blinked for a solid minute. An adult had just admitted something beyond belief. Did he hear Coach correctly?

"There are nine creators?"

"No. Nine parts of one creator. Together they form the creator."

"We're living on a part of God? We've enslaved God himself?" Trib asked, unable to believe such words were coming from his mouth. Standing, he ran his fingers through his hair. This was bigger than he imagined. It didn't seem real.

"I didn't say you could put him back together. No one knows that. These pieces are like pieces of his body. God died and left them behind. If you were split into nine pieces, would putting them back together help? The cities thrive off the remnants of God."

God was dead? But Trib had seen Him. Or a part of Him. He wasn't sure how that worked, but the man inside the Source was very much alive.

"But He spoke to me."

"Did He ask to be freed?"

"No. He was trying to save the planet."

"Then let Him. Do you know better than God? Even a part of Him?"

"You have a point. He just seemed like He was in so much pain."

"So, God feels pain and can't help himself? Sounds a little farfetched, doesn't it?"

It did. Was Trib going down the wrong direction? Following the wrong path? No. Whether it was God, a part of God, or an alien species, it was slavery, and he was going down the right road.

"Thanks, coach. You made it so much clearer."

"Glad to help, son."

He might have been glad to help, but he was pushing the same line of crap that his dad had. Coach Xius tried to persuade Trib in the futility of his...quest? Yeah, it was a quest, and it was his. Trib clenched his jaw. No one was going to stop him. He was Tribinius Cantus, and no one stops the Trib.

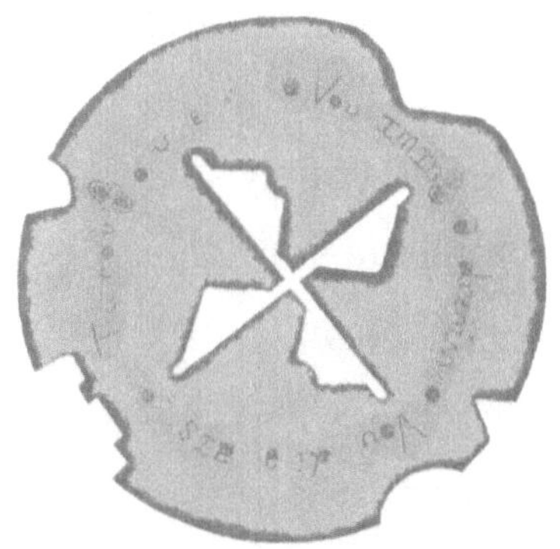

CAN'T STOP THE TRIB

"I don't know what the hell is wrong with their thinking, but slavery is wrong. God should have a choice, even if we don't know why he can't just force his choice," Trib said. "We're going in."

"Ain't waiting peacefully," Ahnd said.

"Good thing we've got you, then."

"Trib, this is going to require some planning. They're going to change all the codes and everything," Liv said.

"And a good thing we've got you, then."

"Sure this is good?" Ahnd asked.

"Yeah. More sure than I have been in a long time."

"And you're not manic, right?" Liv asked.

"No, but I don't think I'd tell you if I were—I wouldn't know it."

"What's next?" Ahnd said.

"We're going to make a show of it. They're going to try to stop us with everything they've got, and we're going to teach them that you can't stop the Trib." He smirked. "Team Trib."

"How?" Liv asked plainly.

That was a good question. Trib hadn't had time to think about it.

"Break it down into the elements," Liv said

"What elements?"

"Your dad's henchmen, getting into the building, getting the Ementhian..." she said, trailing off and throwing her hands up.

"I could freeze them," Trib said. "Pej and his team."

"First rule, no one dies," Ahnd grunted.

"Well, then, what are we going to do?"

Ahnd shrugged, but Liv pulled around and hopped in her recliner, flinging on her visor. She manipulated the Ementhium vapor into the shape of Ementhe Enterprises. Releasing some vapor into the air, the Ementhium solidified.

"Maybe we could trap them in the mailroom?" Liv suggested.

"How? We'd have to have a distraction. Something that could get them all down there. What could do that?"

"You," Ahnd said. "Pure Ementhium. Make shit solid. Hologram?"

"Yeah. I suppose. Why?"

Ahnd swiveled in his chair, flinging his feet onto the

footrest, then flung the seat forward and jumped up.

"Gonna love this," Ahnd said.

The plan took three weeks to finalize. Every detail had to be considered. Ahnd wanted backup plans too, so they had asked themselves where it would go wrong and how, then came up with ways to thwart those. They talked themselves to death. There was no way they could cover every situation. They just had to know it well enough.

With their suits filled with every vapor, they were ready. Trib still had pure Ementhium in him, and didn't fill up with it because he didn't want to water it down. He hoped that was a good choice. In the end, the plan was simple: Distract his dad's lackeys, disable them, get the Ementhian, then race to the bottom and free God.

"This is it. This is our plan," Trib said. "It isn't perfect, but no plan will be. We can make this work."

"It'll take a week to train you. We should go in a week," Ahnd said.

They pushed everything in the living room aside and drew a circle in vapor to define the fight zone. It was Trib vs Liv, and Trib was at a loss. He couldn't hit the girl he loved. She must have felt the same way because she hadn't thrown a punch.

"Fight. Got gloves. Not gonna hurt," Ahnd said.

Apparently, they waited too long. Ahnd stepped into the circle and swung his foot forward and back as he threw his arm out across Liv's chest. When his foot came back and took out her leg, she tumbled backward. Fortunately, he'd positioned himself to catch her and set her gently on the ground.

"Opponent ain't gentle. Want Liv hurt? Fight!"

Trib got up, put up his fists, then leaped at Liv, taking a soft swing at her head. He hit her; she took the hit head on. She glared at him, clenching her teeth, her eyes dilated to a dot. She threw a hard punch, taking him in the ribcage and winding him.

Trib stumbled back, trying to catch his breath.

"You hit me!" Liv said.

"To save you," Trib said.

"Well, here. Let me save you some more," she said, swinging.

Trib put his hands up to block the punches. She was stronger than he thought. That made him a little proud. He started blushing, still dodging her hits, then Ahnd jumped in.

"Enough. Playing fair. Nothing's fair. Fight me. Just pulled her hair and smacked that pretty little face into knee," Ahnd said to Trib.

That was graphic, Trib thought. *Why'd he have to*

go there? Just the idea got Trib going. Who did Ahnd think he was? Training them like this?

Trib raised his fists and came at Ahnd. Ahnd kicked him in his metallic knee, sending him catapulting forward, then brought his fist up and took Trib in the chin. Hard.

When Trib woke up a few minutes later, Ahnd was glaring at him. It was like he wanted to pick a fight with Trib. Ahnd was challenging Trib. Trib rose to the occasion, pushing himself up off the ground with his mechanical arm and raised his fists.

Ahnd relaxed and smiled. It put Trib at ease.

Without changing his expression, Ahnd lunged at Trib. Trib raised his arm to block the swing while Ahnd's other arm came up and punched him in the gut.

Trib coughed and groaned. He could smell blood in his nose from when he was knocked out, but could he now taste it? Ahnd was fighting hard.

Trib raised his fists, then Ahnd laughed and reached out, cupping Trib's hands.

"Don't lose ain't gonna win," Ahnd said.

"What?" Liv said.

"What do you mean?" Trib said, agreeing.

"Don't win, but don't lose. Give up. Better than losing."

"I can't give up this, Ahnd," Trib said.

"Give up me."

"Okay. Teach me."

Ahnd started with a fighting stance, then moved on to dodging; it was better not to get hit. He progressed to blocking, then punches. The repetition was draining, especially for Liv since her arm and leg muscles grew tired. Ahnd was amazing. It was like he had been trained, not picked up things on the street. Midweek, Trib asked about it.

"How'd you learn all this?"

"Mostly Capo."

"What's that mean?"

"Capo's dude."

"Oh, okay. I'd like to meet him one day."

Ahnd shrugged.

"Show what learned," he ordered.

Trib and Liv took a sigh, then entered the fight zone, hands up, one leg back, both knees bent. Liv swung first. She was fast and already had some skills she picked up from her father. Trib didn't see it coming fast enough, so he swung his arm out and blocked, not dodging, then swung for her.

Liv ducked, then punched forward, aiming for Trib's gut, but he jumped back, then looked at his back foot to make sure it was still in the circle. When he looked back at Liv, it was right into her fist. She jabbed him in the nose. Trib winced, but fought back the pain as he grabbed her arm, eyes watering, and jerked her forward, delivering an uppercut to the ribs.

Trib never hit her with his full strength. The force along with his artificial limbs would crack bones, if not worse. She took the hit and coughed.

"Done," Ahnd said.

He moved onto foot training while making them practice everything they learned so far. Near the end of the week, he covered dirty street fighting. They learned about biting, distractions, gouging, weak points on the body, and more. It was beginning to be too much for Trib, but Liv was eating it up and already knew a surprising amount. Had she been playing gently with Trib?

Ahnd pointed at Liv. "Fight me."

They stepped into the fight zone and took their stances. Ahnd attacked first, throwing a kick straight at Liv's face. She ducked and he retracted his foot, but as he pulled back, she charged forward to deliver a hook to Ahnd's ribs, but he pushed with his other foot, throwing his body into a spin and came behind her, wrapping an arm around her neck and holding.

She delivered an elbow to his ribcage and threw her head toward his hand, trying to free her neck, but Ahnd had her locked in place, so she flipped her hands up, thumbs first and went to the eye gouge.

Ahnd released her and returned to his fighting stance. When she turned around, he said, "Good. Trib?"

Liv smiled with pride, then let Trib take her place.

At the ready in their fighting stances, Ahnd attacked Trib with a side kick to the face, but Trib dodged and grabbed his foot. They hadn't been taught that, but it seemed like a good way to throw Ahnd off balance.

Ahnd leveraged the hold and spun his body horizontally, whipping his free foot through the air and hit Trib's head, making his ear ring. Trib shook his head as Ahnd landed on the ground, then swept his foot around, taking out Trib's legs.

Trib crashed down on his back, the wind knocked out of him, and gasped. Ahnd stood and immediately sent a kick at Trib's ribcage, but Trib had had enough. He caught the foot and jerked Ahnd forward, throwing his fist up and stopping just short of Ahnd's nuts.

"Good," Ahnd said. "Ain't playing fair. Gonna fight and lose not using vapor. Hand fighting's last thing to do. Careful grabbing."

Trib wasn't the best fighter, but he was no longer the worst, and Liv was an even better fighter. Ahnd was right, though. Trib hoped he didn't have to use anything he'd learned.

Tomorrow was the day of reckoning. One way or another, his world was about to change.

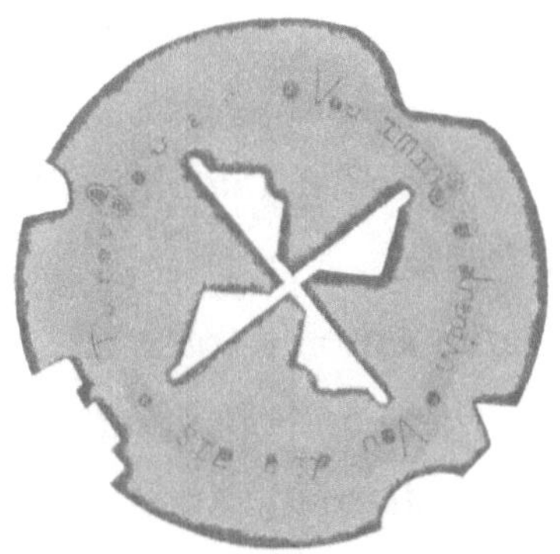

CREATOR CONVERSATION

"Suit check," Trib said. They each looked at their Inves' wrist. Trib's, like the rest, showed a little of each vapor. Not the tenth, of course. That said, they each had a little over 100 reyes of each vapor. They wouldn't be working miracles, but they would have the entire toolbox to use.

"Check," Liv said.

"Check," Ahnd said. "Weapons check."

They each had a knife and two Grop bombs, but those were to be used as a last resort. Ahnd was going to take care of the big bad uglies if everything went as planned. The weapons were for when the plan didn't go well.

"Camera check," Liv said. She peeked into Peetie's eyes. "He's good, too."

"Check," Trib said.

"Check," Ahnd said.

Liv reached out and cast a Brumenium shield around

herself and Ahnd, and they vanished.

"We're a go," Trib said.

"*No. Don't go. You'll get caught,*" said the girl's voice in Trib's mind.

"*I agree,*" came Anton's voice.

Trib ignored them and opened the door, paused for a moment, then turned around and turned out the lights. He closed the door and walked confidently past the commercial buildings and toward Ementhe Enterprises.

The behemoth Avery marched out into the street, huffing and puffing. "Cantus! It's you and me now. None of your little friends around to help you. Going to call for Daddy or ready to be my girl?"

"Avery. I thought we had settled this. Truce, right?"

"Truces are for children and warriors. I'm just the guy that's going to kick your ass."

Trib struck a pose, keeping his knees bent and his arms up, employing everything Ahnd had shown him. Peetie extended his wings and glowed as he transformed into a bearded vulture. He lifted his head and screeched into the air, then ducked his head down to challenge Avery.

"Bring it on, old man!" Trib said.

Cars. He sent them in cars again. Why now, about a block from the building, and not when Trib had been all beaten up? Again, the same entourage, and Pej stepping out in his cool, collected way. The cars wouldn't stop him. He had plans for with and without cars. The cars gave better chances of the next round succeeding.

"I'm thinking I didn't make myself clear. You get to keep your knees and elbows so long as Mr. Cantus here remains untouched."

Rain started falling. It quickly became a deluge, but Pej cocked his head as he noticed something about the rain. It wasn't falling over Avery and Trib. Trib lifted his hand and a bright blue stream burst up out of him. The bright explosion of vapor dimmed, exposing rain frozen in place, streams of rain were solidified into metal.

"Cantus?" Pej said, rather annoyed.

"Thanks, Avery. I told you you'd get back at somebody," Trib said.

"Those are good somebodies. They won't freeze to death, will they?"

"No. I've learned. They'll just be stuck there for a very long time."

The rain, in fact, was not falling everywhere except around Avery and Trib, it was falling only around Pej and his team, and now it formed a metal barrier that locked them all in place. While Trib walked around the enclosure, one of the guards got in the car and tried to back over the steel rods, shredding the trunk of the car.

Peetie stayed perched in full bearded vulture form on

Trib's shoulder as they entered the mailroom. Trib made for the elevator to his father's office, quickly pressing his palm to the device. It opened. Stepping in, he pressed the button for the top floor.

He wasn't sure why his father needed an escape elevator that was so easy to commandeer, but it was convenient for Trib. Most people, of course, didn't even know it existed. His father might reconsider his thoughts about the elevator in about three minutes.

The elevator door opened and Trib paused for a second, then stepped into the room, walking straight over to the hanging Ementhian. He took a deep breath and said, "No going back now, Liv. I love you."

"I love you too," her invisible self whispered.

Trib swiftly pulled the glass case from the wall, then paused, waiting for the alarm bells. He was being foolish. There weren't any alarm bells the first time. It was a silent alarm. He released a little Ementhium from his suit onto the glass case, then hardened it, causing the glass to shatter. The Ementhian fell, and...

Trib caught the Ementhian.

A bright blue light splashed the room, giving Liv a shadow. It came to life, sucking pure Ementhium out of his body and into the Ementhian. The only problem with this was that he wasn't sure how it worked. He concentrated for a moment and tried to focus on building a wall in front of him. The Ementhian didn't obey. It did nothing other than continue melding with Trib.

Peetie squawked and fluffed his feathers, perturbed at the Ementhian.

"Take it, Liv," Trib said, and it quickly disappeared out of his hands.

"Got it," she whispered.

The doors opened and a dozen guards filled the room.

Trib tapped on his Inves, changing the source of vapor, and released a pink vapor into the air, followed by a light blue directly from his fingertips. The blue pushed the pink onto the guards, then exploded and caused the pink Bodigium to generate a stasis field, locking the guards in place.

Trib took his headpiece off and turned it to face him, looking directly into the remote camera Ahnd had installed.

"Hi, friends. Today's a special show. Today we're going to see exactly what a corporation is. It starts with me claiming my birthright: the Ementhian. To see where it ends, stay tuned."

Trib put his helmet back on, then went to the wall, activated the AIR, and cut a hole through the wall. They walked out past the frozen guards and worked their way over to the elevator shaft. The elevator door opened and a bright blue burst of light flew past Ahnd into the elevator. The elevator exploded in light, then tipped over on its side, lodging itself in the shaft.

Peetie hissed and took to flight, angling around at the attacker, claws out.

"I knew you weren't ready. I told your mother you were too weak. Life has been too easy for you. You run around saying you're bipolar to use it as an excuse to cause problems," Caran Cantus said, his words dripping with disgust.

"Dad? What are you doing? You could have killed me."

"I still might. Give back the Ementhian. Give up this quest to free it."

"I can't, Dad. I can't. This is the right thing to do."

A soft, light rain fell. Trib rubbed it between his fingers. It was ash. It was then that he realized what was happening, but Caran was too fast and had Liv by the neck.

He said something next, but Trib's mind didn't register it. There was something about a girl getting hurt, something about a wrong being done, something that triggered him. His heart raced, his breathing grew faster, the red in his eyes burst at the seams. It was Liv. His Livia.

Peetie lunged forward, but Trib was faster.

"No," Trib yelled and thrust his hand out. It burst with an explosion of pure Ementhium that pierced straight through Liv's clothes and gripped the device. He jerked back and the Ementhian flew to him. Vapor curled around him and into the Ementhian. Trib was no longer thinking, just acting. His mind had taken control and somehow by not thinking about it, by not being able to think about it, he *felt* the Ementhian. It called out to him in a melody of vapors that were in time with the Earth, and Trib understood it. It was a song of offering. It was offering itself to him.

Trib opened his eyes. They glowed a bright blue as if his entire body had been consumed by pure Ementhium. A beam of vapor shot out from each eye and wrapped around his father's wrist. The vapor exploded and his hand vaporized.

"You think you're God," Trib said to his father, levitating into the air and pulling on all the Ementhium nearby.

"I will show you God's power."

Trib sucked in pure Ementhium, pulling it fast and hard, then funneled it through the Ementhian, filling the device with power. The tube funneling Ementhium up the tower exploded, releasing a pool of Ementhium that crested above Trib's head. The wave knocked him over and he crashed headfirst into a wall. The Ementhian protected him from the hit, but it threw him off.

Peetie angled and pulled up, flying above the wash of vapor.

He looked around for his father, but he wasn't where he had been. Where would he go? The Source. Trib swam down the center of the shaft and into the Source's cavern. His father stood there defiant and holding the stub of his missing hand.

Trib couldn't do anything while caught in the sea of Ementhium, so he harnessed the Ementhian to create a bubble of air between him and his father. He ducked as Peetie burst through the pool and into the bubble.

"You're a fool, Tribinius. Freeing it will do nothing but destroy us."

Another bubble of air touched Trib's and merged together at the same time that Ahnd and Liv crashed in.

"You can't free him," came a calm, friendly voice from a white-clad man.

Coach Xius?

"I saw your stream, Tribinius. You can't do this. You will literally destroy the world. Ask the Creator. Don't believe me."

Trib jerked an arm off, set it down, and leaned into the sphere. Peetie flew up and hovered in place, half watching Trib, half watching Caran.

"Creator?" Trib said to the naked blue man feeding vapor into the crystal.

"What is it? I'm saving the world."

"If I free you, do we all die?"

"Yes. Look," he said, then suddenly stopped and looked Trib straight in the eyes. His eyes were swirling windows into another place. Trib got lost in them, then found himself seeing through them. He could see the entire planet and a white weave undulating back and forth across the surface of the planet like a wave stuck in place. And he felt the man's unfathomable sadness; he was trapped, hopeless, bound by this network.

"What is it?"

"The gate of the tenth vapor. All nine at once and we survive. Otherwise, the tenth will destroy everything."

Trib pulled back.

As expected, his father had tried to make a go of it when Trib was out, but now he found himself with a scratched face squirming under Ahnd's blade while Liv scowled behind him and a very irritated Peetie flew nearby.

"He's right. Coach is right. It's a trap. If I free him, then we all die."

"Then what do we do?" Liv asked.

"Free them all," Trib said. "I'm keeping the Ementhian, Dad. It's mine now. And we're going to act like none of this happened."

Trib pointed at the pool of Ementhium outside of him and started spinning his finger around. The Ementhium pooled and spun up through the shaft, then the glass shards which had once formed the funneling tube resealed back into place.

"I need to rest now," Trib said. The world went black and he collapsed.

REPLAY

Liv rolled her eyes and sighed. "Now what do we do?"

"Gonna leave," Ahnd said.

"It won't be that easy," Caran said with disdain that only hardened as Ahnd pressed the knife closer.

"What do you mean?" Liv asked.

"I'm not going to stop you, so Mr. Mesixia can unleash me. Do I look fit enough to stop you?"

Liv laughed, then blushed at her rudeness. "It's what Trib wants, Mr. Cantus."

"He doesn't know what he wants. He's a fool that is going to get us all killed. Someone has to stop him. He won't listen to me. Maybe he will listen to you."

"Ain't easy?" Ahnd asked, directing the conversation back to the point.

"Observant, but that's for you to find out." Caran shook himself, and Ahnd relaxed his grip, letting Caran jerk free. "There are powers here bigger than you can imagine. Ask your coach."

Liv looked where Coach Xius had been, but he was gone. He sure was a mystery. Why did he keep showing up, then disappearing at just the right time?

"It's Team Trib," Liv said. "You can't stop us."

"I thought my wife taught you some class. Seems like she has a long way to go."

That struck a chord in Liv. She straightened her posture and looked down past her nose at Caran. "She taught me the value of a person. You," she said, looking toward the source, "seem like you have a long way to go."

Caran huffed.

Ahnd studied the space around, then spawned a hoverboard, worked Trib's appendages off, then heaved Trib onto his back. Nodding to the prosthetics signaled Liv to pick them up. She did and spawned her own hoverboard.

Caran Cantus sighed and left, leaving them to Trib's recovery.

Back at the Pad, they put Trib down to rest and set his arms and legs nearby.

Liv got to work. Trib wasn't going to act like nothing had happened. He said they were going to free them all, and she didn't doubt he meant it for a second. That meant she needed answers when he woke.

The world wouldn't know the truth about the corporations. A frustrated Liv gave up trying to recover data from the corrupted stream. From Caran's attack on the elevator to Trib's last stand was a static blur. She'd tried filters and different mixes of vapor, but nothing could recover the image from any of their headsets.

She pulled her visor off, then slid off her chair and headed to Trib's room. For weeks he had not gotten out of bed except to go to the bathroom. He'd grown a scraggly, attractive beard, but other than that, he hadn't wanted to speak to anyone. Liv was worried that another depressive episode had landed on him.

"Liv," a scratchy voiced Trib said.

Liv lifted her head higher and beamed with delight. Trib was up. Trib, her boyfriend, was coming back to life! He was finally coming back to her. She cupped her hands together in nervous excitement.

"I'm sorry," he said.

"It's okay, Trib. Go shower. You'll feel better. You'll certainly smell better. That attractive musky scent wore off a couple of weeks ago—now you just stink."

Trib showered and came back with a towel around his waist as he dried his hair. Seeing him half naked made her blush for wanting him.

"How's my sexy man?" she said.

"A little better," he said, not picking up on the flirt. "I

just don't know what I'm going to do. We had things so well prepared, then my camera…Oh, that's right. That was my camera we were looking at. Did anyone check Peetie's?"

For a moment, Liv thought it was so obvious that, duh, we checked everything, but searching her memories, she didn't recall ever actually pulling Peetie's footage.

"Peetie," she said, holding out her finger.

The bird with mechanical dragon wings flew to her, then she bent his head back and opened him up, extracting the camera disk. She put him back together again, then shook her finger to send him back to Trib. She slipped the disk into her headset, cued it to play at three times speed, and broadcast it into a cloud of Ementhium.

It was all there. A little bouncy as Peetie hopped, dodged, and flew, but it was still all there.

"Good," a still-deflated Tribinius said. "Now, at least I know what to do."

"Broadcast?" Ahnd asked.

"No. Blackmail. First, I need to talk with Coach."

"Yeah. What's up with him? Why was he there?" Liv said.

"He isn't who he says he is."

Councilor Cantus swore that the sphere was brighter than usual. The Leader's tone confirmed his irritation.

"No one is to touch a Source. Not even you."

"But we all have," Caran interrupted, reflexively looking at his missing hand. He had a prosthetic in place now, but he swore he could feel his fingers at times and it still hurt as his body adjusted to it.

The sphere glowed whiter, but Caran wasn't about to back down. Not now. It meant too much.

"Questions were raised about your son. You have ignored them, and I have allowed them too long. You are stripped of your vote on the Council until you get the Ementhian back *and* you get your son under control."

"My vote? What about a tie? This is unfair. I did nothing wrong."

Councilor Plourvald snorted, and Caran gave him a quick glare.

"If you do not rein him in soon, further action will be taken."

The Leader stepped back into the light. Caran felt cold. Isolated from his peers, thrown out of his own house, stripped of his power. He was less than all of them. And all because of his son. He would bring that son of a bitch to heel or die trying.

Trib stepped into the gym, and Coach Xius immediately noted him, giving him a nod and a finger up to indicate he would be right over. Coach sent the class on a run around the track, then jogged over to Trib.

"Who are you?" said Trib.

Coach Xius flipped his chin, signaling Trib to save it for his office. In his office, Coach took a seat and offered Trib one, but Trib remained standing.

"Your choice. Might as well be comfortable. I'm the forgotten heir. Alexander Reyes didn't have nine children, he had nine daughters. He had one son, a son who was left out of the corporations. I'm Alexander Reyes' great-great-grandchild through his son."

"What vapor did he give you? Your great grandfather?"

"The tenth. I'm the castaway, but I still feel a need to protect what my great-great-grandfather created. I had to come help you and save you from destroying us all. What kind of legacy would that leave behind?"

It made sense, but there was something disingenuous about it. He was holding something back, almost like he was hiding the truth in the truth.

"Thanks, Coach. Can I still trust you?"

"I never said you could, Trib. You said that. I have my own motivations. You can trust that, and so long as my motivations don't cross with yours, you can trust me."

The only people Trib trusted now were Liv and Ahnd. He couldn't even trust Coach anymore. Well, Team Trib was still together, and that meant that they were

going to get all nine medallions. They were going to free
God.

Thank You

Thank you for reading The Ementhian. I hope you enjoyed it! You can find out more information about this series on my website.

https://sylas.art

Please take a moment and review your read on Amazon or GoodReads—your reviews are an enormous help to authors.

amazon.com/dp/B0CZ4CRPC9

goodreads.com/book/show/205225779-the-ementhian

Newsletter

For freebies and to stay abreast of all my new works, please sign up for my newsletter:

https://sylas.art/signup

More From Sylas Seabrook

Pure Impurity
Now Available

A prophecy divides a world and masks a war between those with the power to create life and those who covet it. We weather the impending destruction of Earth, survive a doomed planet, and ride the tide of a planet's last age while following the conflict to its inevitable conclusion: a battle for harmony that rocks the very foundations of Existence.

A woman so passionately in love with her husband spends thousands of years in search of him. A creature gives up its home in the desperate hope of saving their species. A fascinated scientist discovers what lies beyond our universe. And a son abandoned by his father seeks to return and take his place as rightful heir. Pure Impurity takes you on a journey like no other to discover the greatness in all of us.

The Rise Of Tribinius Cantus
Coming 2024

Tribinius Cantus, a bipolar 16-year-old born without his limbs, discovers an 1100-year-old secret hidden by the Corporation he's destined to control. He's forced to question everything he knows. God or aliens? Slavery or freedom? Faith or reason?

He fights his bipolar ups and downs while setting out on an impossible quest. A quest to unravel the mystery and save humankind.

Pursued by police, hunted by Corporations, his friends will suffer and his family will be crushed. He will pay an unimaginable price for his beliefs, driven by a deep understanding of loneliness and hopelessness.

Giving up will seem to be his only option.

But humanity has one hope. A hope that runs deep in Trib. A belief that will push him on, pick him up, and take him to new heights.

There's one thing his enemies need to know: you can't stop the Trib.

Pure Impurity Books

Arter
Ertra
Terra
The Universum

Novelettes

The Trasilian War
The Sareman Silence

The Rise of Tribinius Cantus Books

The Ementhian
The Tarian
The Tituerian
The Mæssian
The Seignian
The Bodigian
The Brumenian
The Triusian
The Groppian
The Dian
Jarev Reyes

Novella

Ahnd